THE
BIRTHMARK

Books by Dorothea Straus

Thresholds
Showcases
Palaces and Prisons
Under the Canopy
The Birthmark

THE BIRTHMARK

A NOVEL

Dorothea Straus

GEORGE BRAZILLER NEW YORK

Published in the United States in 1987 by
George Braziller, Inc.
Copyright © 1987 by Dorothea Straus

George Braziller, Inc.
60 Madison Avenue
New York, New York 10010

Library of Congress Cataloging-in-Publication Data

Straus, Dorothea.
  The birthmark.

   I. Title.
PS3569.T6918B5   1987   813′.54   87-713
ISBN 0-8076-1174-3

Book design by Helen Granger/Levavi & Levavi
Printed in the United States of America
First printing, April 1987

PART 1

GREEN MEADOWS

IT HAD BEEN MY INTENTION TO TELL THE STORY OF
Nicholas. But, unbidden, my own past intruded
and in searching out my brother, I, also, discover
myself. I see us, side by side, like the silver mugs
that used to stand on the nursery shelf. For some
mysterious reason they remain, shining, in memory; although physically they have been lost for
ages in the detritus of another era. Gifts to celebrate
our births (Nicholas made his appearance in this
world just eighteen months before me), the cups
were engraved with our names and the date; shortly
after World War I. From all accounts, that event left
our family comparatively uninvolved; our father
being overage and his Germanic upbringing having
prevented him from despising the Kaiser with proper
American fervor. In his childhood home within the
courtyard of the ancestral business—Joseph Bloch
and Sons, Breweries, which had been transported
in 1848 from Ludwigsburg to Brooklyn—German
had been his first language. Our mother's forebears
emigrated during the same period, becoming prosperous Manhattan merchants. Our parents, both

products of the Enlightenment, shunned all dog-matic faiths, Father a militant atheist, Mother un-able to rid herself of a tentative attraction toward some unaffiliated mysticism. But as assimilated German Jews, they were united in their deliberate ignorance of Jewish religion, culture and history. The silver mugs, portentous in recall, had no ritual significance. But, in my childhood, they were al-ways referred to as "loving cups," conjuring up in my imagination stories of banqueting among the bonded fraternity of King Arthur's Knights of the Round Table. It is probable that the cups were so called merely because of their rotund shapes and their double handles for infant fingers to grasp at their suppers of milk and porridge. But it was a misnomer, for, as far back as I can remember, I chose *not* to love my brother, to dissociate myself from him, to dwell upon our differences—to dis-avow our consanguinity. . . . But that is part of the life history of Nicholas Bloch, which, whether I wish it or not, is indissolubly linked to my own.

ONE

A first home, like the person who arouses our initial awakening to sex, holds forever strong sway over our emotions that no later experience or grander house is able to eclipse. With the precision of a blueprint, I can locate and reassemble every room, each nook and corner at Green Meadows. And all places and objects are related to a particular actor in that theatre of time passed. In the living room, always shaded against the heat spells of Westchester County summers, my mother can be found at her piano. I have no difficulty turning the knob of that double door on the right side of the large entrance hall, or recognizing the comfortable eighteenth-century English furniture within. I see the carpet, the color of ripe mulberries, the face of the grandfather clock, a full moon in the perpetual evening of the living room. My mother is less distinct, her pale beauty a phantom in the obscurity. But I hear the discreet click of her fingernails on the keyboard as she plays her favorite German Romantic composers or accompanies herself as she sings her beloved lieder in a modest, true voice. Generous and unpretentious, she wished to include her family in her passion for music. Sometimes, in the evenings, we would gather in the living room, with the shades raised, the order of things reversed and the room glowing in the rose-gold light of the setting sun. For those family recitals, my mother usually selected jolly, rollicking tunes from Gilbert and Sullivan operettas and Negro spirituals. "Old Black Joe" was a familiar; we all sang out, "I'm coming, I'm coming, though my head is bending low, I hear those gentle voices calling 'Ol Black Joe.' . . ." I invariably saw the Pullman porter who waited on us during our train trips to the Adirondacks, his cropped, grizzled, kinky hair, ebony face and back stooped from making up so many cozy berths for others. At the call of death, he would appear as sweet-natured and compliant as when summoned by the ring of the compartment bell. During these homemade concerts, my father, tone deaf, was cooperatively silent, but Nicholas, voluble and restless, often interrupted to beg for a new toy or permission to stay up past the usual hour for bed. "Give me . . . I want . . . I won't . . ." were insistent refrains.

"Hush dear, let us finish," my mother said.

But her words were ineffectual in stemming the flood of demands.

"Make him leave the room." I even tried to push him, twice my size, away from his place near the piano.

But my show of temper was of no more avail than my mother's gentle reproof. My father often dozed peacefully during these family crises.

But there was one occasion on which I welcomed Nicholas's irrepressible eruptions. It was when my mother turned up a certain English ballad and I heard, once more, the dread lament: ". . . I'm tying the leaves so they won't fall down so Nelly won't go away . . ."

"I want the money to buy it tomorrow . . . it only costs . . ."

The words of the song, so gently mournful, exploded in my head. Nelly, a little girl, lay dying. . . . I might die also. . . . It might happen to me . . . during a late summer, sunny and lush, like the season in which Nelly was fading away, while a loving friend or relation was trying, in vain, to hold back nature in order to postpone the moment of the little invalid's succumbing. My mother's soft, familiar voice was powerless to soothe my terror. It was possible for me to die, too!

". . . the kit has a magic wand, trick cards and disappearing coins. . . ."

I prayed that Nicholas would not stop and that the song would be discontinued. If he were opposed there might be one of those hysterical scenes which would cleanse the atmosphere of my melancholy. But Nelly's song would show up again and again in our repertory. In the autumn I averted my eyes from the falling leaves and my spirits did not salute the hoisting of the flamboyant scarlet, gold and bronze flags waving from the trees. I would not confess my fears, I knew that children were meant to be happy all the time, it was their duty —unless they were "queer," and I aspired to be regular like everyone else. And, most vehemently,

I wished to be unlike my brother who was different, loud and uncontrolled. In the evenings, my mother also read to us: *The Wind in the Willows*, *Alice in Wonderland*, *Peter Pan*. Of course Nicholas was unable to sit still; the stories so absorbing to me did not interest him. Yet it was he who had learned to read fluently before he was five years old. His favorite fare was railroad schedules, pamphlets from the luxury steamship lines and F. A. O. Schwartz catalogues. I, at a later age, was still struggling with bland, sunbonneted "Fanny," who had an "apple," pretending to decipher the large print, while actually improvising from the illustrations.

My father's dressing room adjoined my parents' bedroom. It waited all day for his return from the city. His tweed jacket was fitted across the wooden shoulders of a clothes rack; beneath it, his polished boots with high uppers were at readiness to spring into action when my father vaulted nimbly onto the saddle for his early-morning or late-afternoon ride. In the closet his ties were suspended in a rainbow cascade and his pin-striped white flannels and blazers were a chorus line in order for the show to start. On the bureau, in place of honor, were photographs of his parents, venerable and severe. My father had inherited his mother's fleshy nose and small, wise eyes, but in his face they looked pleasingly elfin, while the old woman in the portrait (whom I had never seen) resembled an ancient turtle wrapped in a soft wool shawl. My white-haired, white-bearded grandfather was as I remembered him on Sunday visits in the wintertime: broad and solid as a stein of beer topped by the proud snowy crest like the Blochs' famous beer foam. These photographs were never moved from their appointed positions and they were impressive because they commanded my father's respect; more so, perhaps, than the old gentleman of flesh and blood who required the gathering of his progeny at regular occasions and who stolidly continued to read his German periodicals through a magnifying glass while his sons, daughters and in-laws tried to entertain him with their forced chatter.

The bench beneath the tall window on the landing midway up the stairs that rose in graceful double–branching curves from the hall was my special place. It overlooked a small brick-walled flower garden, enclosed as another room. Against the stones, pink, red and white hollyhock stood sentinel. It was here on the seat on the landing that I kept house with my dolls, enjoying the snugness, suspended over the large open area below. Later, just as inside a church a worshipper is hypnotized into glimpsing heavenly realms through the prisms emanating from stained glass, the light through the clear panes of the window on the staircase was empowered to transport me, via the book I was reading, to exotic lands and people.

Only Nicholas, my brother, can claim no section in the map of that house. But I remember a snapshot of us together taken during my first summer at Green Meadows. It is so real that I still seem to feel the cushions at my back propping me inside the wicker perambulator. Under the hood I sit upright, wearing an embroidered bonnet, my round eyes stare with determination straight ahead, away from the small boy at the side of the carriage, who clutches a handlebar. He has long, fair "Little Lord Fauntleroy" curls and a pretty face marred by a birthmark, like a dark moth, across the bridge of his nose. The occupant of the carriage looks as though she wished to be rid of him; were she able to talk, she might have called him "sissy"—a word out of fashion today. The pose of the innocent infant in the snapshot hints at the hostility contained in an indistinct future.

Green Meadows, an ordinary Georgian type brick suburban house, was once the center of my universe. From it, like the spokes of a wheel, routes extended to other sites. But I would return to our own welcoming front door, and its fanlight window spread like a peacock's tail, with all the pleasure of a wayfarer's homecoming.

The way to the farm, a rural enterprise that my parents abandoned before the sale of Green Meadows itself when I was ten, was bumpy with rocks and muddy ruts. It was in contrast to the raked white gravel driveway encircling the sphere of lawn, plump as an emerald pincushion in front of our house. On either side of the path grass grew, ragged and neglected, dotted with Queen Anne's lace, pink clover, thistles, goldenrod like gypsies camping in the fields. First one came upon the chicken coop, a dry sandy enclosure, an impoverished village square, populated by a feathered citizenry. Only the roosters proudly wearing their scarlet fezzes and the egg-laying hens would escape the fate of the bloody ax. I hated to see the others jostling and greedily pecking at the grain scattered by the hand of Peterson, the farmer, knowing that they were being fattened for the kill. Sometimes Nicholas and I were allowed to gather eggs. But, as a city child, I recoiled from their newly expelled vaguely excremental warmth; they bore no relation to the boiled egg enthroned on its china cup on the breakfast table. Waking in the gray of early morning, I listened to the cock's crow, like a warning siren breaking the silence of the countryside. It was supposed to be educational for Nicholas and me to observe nature, but studying the parts of expensive cars was more to his liking and I was relieved when the smelly doomed chickens were given up, and the coop remained deserted.

Peterson, the tenant farmer, lived at the end of the road. Here was another village square built around a non-functioning well with a rusted pump. This area was sparsely populated, a meeting place for skinny, stray cats, very different from our own household pets. Although these latter never lasted long, during their brief stay with us, they were pampered and petted like spoiled children. There had been the monstrously obese white rabbit who filled to overflowing his outgrown hutch. He died, a bleary, pink-eyed Nero, from overeating and inactivity. We had a canary who could not be coaxed to sing, and goldfish who swam in and out of our lives at various intervals. During one summer at Green Meadows, my brother and I were the possessors of a russet cocker spaniel puppy, named America (Merry, for short). Nicholas loved him extravagantly, addressing him in baby talk, which I found disgusting. "Woof-woof come to your daddy who wuvs you." These excesses made me feign an indifference toward Merry that I was far from feeling. As the dog had never been properly housebroken, when the time came to move back to the city, it was announced that a lovely, permanent home in the country had been found for him. "He will be much happier there," my mother explained, "and we can visit him every summer." But we never did. At the moment of parting Nicholas sobbed hysterically and hugged the squirming animal close. "No, No!" he screamed, "you can't take him from me—I won't let you . . . I will be sick . . . I will not go back without him. . . ." I stood by stonily with a lump in my throat. Our current *Fräulein*, observing my apparent indifference in contrast to the storm of Nicholas's devotion, observed, "*Das Kleine* has a hard heart. She doesn't even care about her puppy." This, despite the fact that she herself was terrified of all dogs and would cringe whenever our harmless pet came near. I smarted at the injustice, while Nicholas continued ranting and raving until the dog had to be forcibly removed from his strangling embrace. Yet it was I who missed Merry for months, thinking I heard his tags jingling when there was only the silence of absence. Surprisingly, Nicholas recovered rapidly from his grief, he referred to Merry cheerfully and with no anxiety about his welfare, absorbed by the acquisition of some new toy or gadget. . . . The farmer's shingle wooden house was ramshackle, the gray paint peeling, the steps up to the rickety porch sagging. Flies swarmed everywhere, entering through holes in the window screens. It was puzzling and depressing that Peterson, so near us and always so friendly and helpful, should live in squalor. I did, however, envy him his barn with its high, fragrant hayloft. I would have liked to make a room for myself there and, like Heidi, dwell under the slanting beams. The stable smelled of fresh milk and dung. At milking time the cows, lined up patiently in their stalls, waited for Peterson to relieve their swollen red udders. Seated on a stool, his head leaning against a rear flank, he manipulated the full inflamed bags, causing the milk to spurt into a pail with a tinny splash. On the opposite side of the stable, my father's black stallion, Woton, was lodged. For a short while, a smaller horse, belonging to Nicholas, was his neighbor. My father was proud to set out accompanied by his son. But his pleasure was of short duration. Nicholas, whose seat on the horse was always precarious, his long legs, without grip, flapping loosely, was thrown and so cruelly stamped upon that he had to have sixteen stitches in his abdomen. I did not witness the accident, but for the rest of his stay in the stable, I would not go near the dangerous beast. I mistrusted his large, wild, vacant bloodshot eyes, his restless stomping, the iron shoes, instruments that had inflicted my brother's wound, ringing out on the stable floor. Although Nicholas never rode again, it was he who timidly approached the animal. Standing outside the half-open door of the stall, I see him, his gangling legs in knickers, his "Little Lord Fauntleroy" curls shorn in deference to his approaching manhood. He is tall for his age and as uncoordinated as a rag doll and there is a frightened, apologetic look in his eyes.

"Open your hand, Master Nicholas," urged Peterson.

Nicholas cautiously unfurled his fingers.

"See, he wants the sugar. Don't be afraid, give it to him," the farmer encouraged.

The horse's inappropriately soft, velvety muzzle reached out for the prize lying exposed on Nicholas's proffered palm. He lifted the lump of sugar off gently, but his long yellow teeth, like saws, pulverized it, saliva foaming at his muzzle. He withdrew his head from the opening. But I had seen them together, supplicant and tormentor. Nicholas looked gratified that his bribe had been accepted, the propitiatory offering had not been spurned. In my mind's eye, the camera clicks at this moment, the portrait of Nicholas has been caught. It will never fade.

Sometimes, instead of following the path to the farm, we set off in the opposite direction, toward the castle of the Thalheims on the hill. The memory of this route dates from earliest childhood, because I see Nicholas and me in the charge of two *Fräuleins*, Clara and Johanna Iske, spinster sisters, one portly, one lean, both flaxen-haired with florid complexions and given to "bad nerves." They spoke English to us and we never learned German, although our parents spoke it fluently, always conversing with our ancient paternal grandfather in a tongue I had heard praised as "High German." It was evidently something to be proud of, the language of the great poets (Goethe and Schiller). Clara and Johanna Iske preferred the walk to the castle, their feudal Teutonic natures causing them to regard with respect this formidable pile of Gothic masonry, carved and turreted, imported stone by stone from England. The Thalheims were enormously wealthy bankers, social leaders in our assimilated German–Jewish society. They lived like lords, and looking back, I realize that my family in our comfortable suburban house was, in relation to them, like gentry to rural nobility. It was no ordinary invitation when they were summoned to the castle for a dinner party. My mother, usually plain in dress, would put on a long gown with a spray of artificial scarlet flowers adorning one white shoulder and an unaccustomed touch of lipstick to match. Around her neck she hung her diamond lavaliere, her only costly jewel (a wedding gift from my father). It was brought out only for "state occasions," from the velvet case where its glitter lay entombed. When she kissed me goodnight, I sensed her happy trepidation, like a young girl's before a first ball. Years later I smarted at this memory of her. My father grumbled inside his stiff summer tuxedo, but submitted. The *Fräuleins*, Nicholas and I were not privileged to enter the castle. As we trudged up the hill in the hot sun, the *Fräuleins* were moved to soulful admiration of the beauties of nature. "God's masterpieces!" they declared. But their brisk commands soon took over. "March quick! It will build strong muscles in the legs." When we arrived before the castle, admiration gave way to awe as they contemplated the princely edifice: the front portico, thick as a grotto, the many small mullioned windows, the crenellated towers, the gradation down to a formal garden which was the work of an army of employees, rather than "God's creation." "*Schön*," Johanna and Clara Iske would declare in unison, clasping their hands as though in prayer. Nicholas always loitered around the garage. He knew the names of all the deluxe automobiles: Pierce Arrow, Isota, Rolls Royce, Daimler. They were the forebears of the expensive cars that later would be his. Rich or bankrupt, my brother required them to bolster his indomitable but shaky ego; actual or not, he had to flaunt wealth. The walk to the Thalheims took us past our playground in the shade of chestnut trees. In early summer they offered their clusters of white blossoms like candelabras, later, the nuts fell to the ground, polished mahogany finials, better than any toy. The playground was fitted out with standard equipment: slide, swing, sandbox and seesaw. I wonder today why a child is meant to prefer the iron treads of a slide to a climb into the branches of a tree, and the gritty confines of a sandbox to the freedom of a field of swaying daisies. Nicholas shrank from the athletic apparatus; he insisted upon holding *Fräulein*'s hand to mount the slide, and someone had to be there to receive him at the bottom, despite the fact that with his long legs he had almost no distance to travel. I was humiliated by his cries for help from his seat on the up end of the seesaw. Sometimes the Thalheim grandchildren (twin sisters, Prudence and Charity, and their younger brother, Geoffrey), descended the hill to join us at our playground. They looked quite commonplace and it relieved my embarrassment to note that Geoffrey was almost as inept and cowardly as Nicholas.

One day in the wooded acreage of the Thalheim estate, we met the patriarch, Leopold, on horseback, accompanied by April, the youngest of his six progeny. He was a familiar sight, with his fierce bushy black mustache and hawk nose, but I had never seen this daughter before. She had been living abroad for several years and was only returning to celebrate her wedding to an English lord at the castle that summer. Leopold Thalheim reined his horse to a halt and April did the same. The two stood side by side, their saddles rubbing against one another with a companionable squeak of leather against leather, as their horses shifted position in place. Leopold Thalheim leaned down from his seat to greet us, the reins slack but controlled in his hands, to introduce his daughter. With one look I took in her goddess form: tall, slim, lithe graceful curves set off by her fitted habit with a long skirt (something I had seen before only in pictures), she was mounted sidesaddle. Beneath her derby her eyes were deep brown pansies, her nose small, disdainful, tip-tilted, her smile slow but radiant, her golden hair, confined, fell in a silken rope to her waist. Father and daughter touched their spurs to the flanks of the horses and were off, cantering out of sight.

"Ach! just like the Emperor Franz Josef and the Empress Elizabeth!" exclaimed Johanna Iske, who suffered from homesickness and decorated her room with picture postcards of the "Old Country."

"Walk, *kinder*," said Clara, for whom physical fitness took precedence over useless dreams of the past.

I rarely saw April after this first encounter, but for years the faces I crayoned in my drawing books, crude and unrecognizable for the most part, had in common one unmistakable feature: that small, impertinent, retroussé nose imprinted on my memory.

It was too far to go to the train station on foot, so Nicholas and I were driven there to meet the five forty-five by Kevin McMullen, the chauffeur. He was like an Irish nanny to us, his robust, good nature a relief from the *Fräuleins*, rigid and humorless, with their chronic nervous complaints. Along the high road we met the billboards advertising their products: Socony tires was represented by a robotlike figure composed entirely of rubber rings of various sizes; Wrigley's Spearmint Gum proclaimed itself through a group of elves in cool green with pointed hats like the pinnacles of pine trees; but Murad cigarettes was recommended by two magnified, totally realistic heads, intimately sharing the flame of a single match. These and others were old friends who hailed us along the way.

White Plains was an unprepossessing adolescent village, rapidly developing into the even more unattractive adulthood of a city. But I savored all the landmarks: we were bound to meet my father. At the bottom of a steep slum street was the station, a brick cube with windows that glittered in the sun like the isinglass perforations in Nicholas's toy depots. But at that hour it had, for me, the proportions of a Greek temple. My father would emerge from the exit, along with all the other men, toilers in the hot city. The locomotive shrieked, the wheels ground to a noisy standstill. And just as the mechanical apostles in a clock tower appear punctually with the striking of the hour, the wilted commuters getting off the five forty-five swarmed toward their waiting cars. There he was! I spotted him at once among the others: small, compact, his butterfly foulard bow tie still in place, his straw boater somehow distinguishable from the rest, his cane an ornament that accompanied his confident, energetic step; a trademark more indigenous than on the billboards, Socony's rubber tire men or the perpetual match flame of Murad cigarettes. Only as he came closer could I see the beads of perspiration, like seed pearls on his swarthy, smooth-shaven upper lip. The warmth of his hug and the damp kisses were compensation enough for having deserted me all day. It is only now, looking back, that I can define the different quality in his love for Nicholas and me. Nicholas, the firstborn, the son, he regarded with Old Testament pride, although, militant atheist that he was, he would have denied this stoutly. He glorified Nicholas from the moment of birth, investing him in the cradle with dynastic dignity; he was to be groomed as chief of the family enterprises. My father would always remain blind to his son's wild excesses, deaf to his hysteria, unresisting to his demands. The father, worldly-wise, moderate, pragmatic, would come to regard his so different offspring as his personal immortality on earth. Small, neat, well-coordinated, he was to look with astonished admiration, mixed with bewilderment and pain, at his awkward six-foot-five creation and, unmatched as the limb might be, Nicholas's right arm he determined should be his. As for me, I was cherished and enjoyed with a light heart. For reasons I never questioned, he would banteringly call me his "mouse." Perhaps the pet name had its origin in my silence when in the proximity of the avalanche of Nicholas's volubility. Although I detested those small slithering creatures, from my father I accepted the name as an endearment, and I rejoiced in it as another indication of my separateness from Nicholas. Just as at the border between two adjacent yet alien nations there is an abrupt change of landscape and language, it was my hope that although I dwelt side by side with my brother, I was securely divided by the frontier of our father's two loves.

When my father's cousin, Daniel Bloch, came for dinner, Nicholas and I again drove with Kevin to fetch him at the Pickwick Arms hotel in Greenwich, Connecticut. My father always spoke of Daniel with contempt, using words that meant little to me, like "spendthrift" and "bankrupt." I knew that Daniel was supported on the charity of Bloch relatives and that it was all due to his "squandering his lavish attentions on fallen women." His generosity in coming to the aid of ladies who had suffered accidents seemed to me to be his credit; but my father was unrelentingly censorious, my mother, pitying. . . . Greenwich was gracious, lined with large, old-fashioned houses, comfortably separated by well-tended grounds and partly concealed by fieldstone walls, giant elms and maples that dappled our way with alternating light and shade.

Daniel lived by himself in the big hotel on Main Street. His choice of location and his solitary state were, according to overheard rumor, the result of his having actually married one of those unsure-footed women, now confined to a nearby sanatorium with an ailment too terrible to be named in my presence, even in the veiled language used to discuss Daniel and his other problems. Secretly, I found him ingratiating, in a grotesque, gnarled way. He reminded me of the nursery rhyme about a crooked man who lived in a crooked house, had a crooked dog and carried a crooked stick . . . etc. Daniel's back was humped, his nose curved down toward his upper lip, and although he smiled frequently, his mouth contorted as though his determined cheerfulness were painful, like his long fingers twisted with rheumatism; he wore his hat at a jaunty, stylish angle. His walking stick, however, was straight and polished like my father's and there was nothing crooked about the Pickwick Arms hotel, a fake Tudor building with geometric crisscrossed wood beams and extensions that covered an entire town block. But Daniel had no dog, no one to care for him and I gathered that this was the reason for my parents' invitation. I was glad to see him and he always carried a box of candy for us. He greeted us in a hoarse rasping voice that used to frighten me when I was little. But I soon found out that there was nothing fierce about him; on the contrary, he was kindly and theatrically chivalrous. Those harsh sounds, like the hard shell of a snail, protected a heart that was vulnerable, tender and sentimental. I looked forward to those evenings when Daniel came for dinner and wondered why the fancy box of chocolates went unappreciated by my parents. They never admired the pink satin ribbon rosettes, nor the sweets inside, wrapped in multicolored tinfoil like a coffer of jewels. Daniel ate sparingly, no wonder he remained sere. But that hoarse rasping voice went on and on, as though it were companionship, not food, that he hungered for.

"How is Maisie feeling?" my mother inquired.

"The same—always the same. I visit her every day, although sometimes she does not even recognize me," Daniel answered. Then changing the subject and turning to my father, he asked, "What's happening at the brewery?"

My father mumbled a few words, grudgingly. He was reluctant to discuss family business with Daniel who had been excluded from all participation in it: because of his being a "black sheep," I surmised.

When I examined him across the table, I decided that, with his curved nose like a single horn and his show of aggressiveness, he did resemble a ram, but I was flattered by his attentions to me. Unlike most adults, he never talked down and he appeared to be genuinely enjoying my company at table.

"That's a nifty frock you are wearing," he might say, or, "This little lady is A-one in my estimation." And—turning to my parents—"You must be very proud of her."

Although my mother and father believed in the open expression of praise for children, they seemed displeased by Daniel's observations and they quickly changed the subject to bland, boring grown-up talk. But, because of Daniel's admiration, my dress, the conventional garb of small girls in our society (puffed-sleeved, smocked, with prim white collar and made from an imported British flowered Liberty print— a copy of the costume of a well-brought-up young Londoner), took on for me the frou frou seductiveness of a ball gown appropriate to one of those "fallen women" he loved.

One summer I overheard through scraps of conversation not meant for my ears (death was never mentioned before children) that Maisie had succumbed, at last. Yet Daniel continued to live at the Pickwick Arms, more isolated than ever—and he still arrived at our house for an occasional dinner. . . . Now he no longer visited the sanatorium but told us that he went to the local cemetery weekly. I pictured him, his hat at the characteristic jaunty angle, placing a bouquet of flowers beneath his wife's headstone, as courtly toward the dead woman as he had been, for so many years, to the living wreck.

Later I discovered an interesting piece of family lore: Daniel, "the black sheep," had made a significant contribution to the brewery. One night in his youth, while attending the opera, carried away by Richard Wagner's *Die Meistersinger von Nürnberg*, he had a sudden inspiration. Already an outcast from J. Bloch and Sons for his irregularities and unreliability, Daniel, nonetheless, admired in this opera the calm wisdom of the industrious shoemaker, Hans Sachs, and the solemn dignity of the members of the guild. His bosom swelled with pride; no matter that he, Daniel Bloch, had been born a Jew, the life of the ghetto, the uneasy placelessness of the Diaspora had, ages past, been expunged from the memories of his forebears. Chauvinistic German tears welled in Daniel's eyes as he sat in a box in New York's Metropolitan Opera House and reached out blindly to hug the object nearest to him; the beruffled lady by his side. He received a strong whiff of sickly sweet perfume as she snuggled closer, hoping that this demonstration of emotion might lead to another trinket from Tiffany. But, at this moment, Daniel was oblivious to his companion; instead of *Violets in the Rain*, he was smelling the odor of malt brew. During the final act as the Meister Singers moved with pomp and ceremony in time to the powerful beat of the processional music to be followed by the soaring notes of the Prize Song, an epiphany to ideal human love and the solid virtues of the German craftsmen, Daniel exclaimed aloud, "That's it! It shall be the Meister-singer Brewery." And the dull Joseph Bloch & Sons was dropped, the new name adopted and, thanks to Daniel, the medieval guilds of Nürnberg had a commemoration in the twentieth century within a brewery compound in Brooklyn.

It is only in recent years that I have understood why a bit player out of my childhood, a distant cousin who came for dinner only rarely, always leaving tactfully at an early hour, remains in my memory. Genes, like pollen sown on the wind, turn up again at random, in distant places. And some of Daniel's characteristics were transplanted and perpetuated in the remote loam of Nicholas's nature. Yet those same traits which I found pictur-esque in Daniel were a source of shame to me in my brother. We do not view people objectively, but bestow upon them the embellishment or disfigure-ments of our fancies, until they become creatures of our own making. Now that both Daniel and Nicholas are gone, questions arise that never oc-curred to me before. And as I hear the echo of these words—". . . idiot . . . optimistic fool . . . not to be trusted . . ."—I realize that, unbeknown to my father, they might be applied, as well, to his son. But it is of Daniel that he speaks, whom I have resurrected in the mellow light of summer evenings at Green Meadows long ago.

TWO

THE COMBINED ODORS OF CHALK DUST, VARNISH, disinfectant and cafeteria foods transport me back to a place that exists only in recall: my first school. Any one of these smells may arouse all the others, so that today, when I pass the open door of a quick-order luncheonette, the stale stench wafted out to the street carries with it a whiff of chalky black-boards, antiseptics and polish. At once I am en-gulfed in a wave of nausea, my stomach heavy with apprehension. And there arises before me the large, gloomy school building, forlorn as an orphanage. In the vast rotunda of the entrance hall, at the top of the stairs, I am confronted each morning by the dazzling white marble, one-armed torso of the *Venus de Milo* with her classical, perfectly formed empty eye sockets. The goddess is my guide into the ob-scurity of this nether world where I am an exile from home only city blocks away.

It remains a puzzle to me why my parents chose this semi-public school, so different from our pro-tected family atmosphere, for Nicholas and me. I can only guess that it was another compromise:

generally barred from what they considered the first class, exclusive private schools, they selected an institution where ethnic and economic groups could mingle in accordance with the American ideal of the melting pot. Yet my parents' liberal impulses must have been mixed and tentative, because my brother and I were inappropriately transported to our democratic place of learning in the family limousine with the faithful Kevin McMullen at the wheel. As we approached the Upper West Side, my heart sank and I wanted to cling to Kevin, to be consoled by his imperturbable benevolence. His chunky frame, broad ruddy face, his beaming blue walleyes straying behind rimless spectacles had, at this time, the comforting glow of calm mother love. I wished never to leave the padded ease of his blessed shelter. But the dreaded moment arrived: Nicholas and I mounted the broad steps together. Even he, for once, was unnaturally silent. Like a spent prisoner before the moment of execution, he knew that it was too late for protest; each morning at home was rent by his loud refusals to leave for school and horrible retching sounds that orchestrated my own suppressed revolt. But Nicholas was ineffectual; my parents, usually permissive, now stood firm. To be a "quitter" was considered a moral stigma (especially for the male sex), it might mark you for the rest of your life. In the entrance hall beneath the blind gaze of the marble Venus, Nicholas and I went our separate ways along the endless corridors permeated, even at this early hour, by the smell of greasy stew from the kitchens.

Miss Robbins presided from a dais, her henna-dyed, old-fashioned pompadour outlined against the chalky blackboard. The letters she inscribed there were multicolored but the numbers were uniformly white lined up in vertical and horizontal lines like an enemy army. The room extended in acres of small, identical wooden desks and chairs soldered into the floor, and the first grade pupils, anonymous as the furnishings, were pinioned into their assigned seats imprisoned by the scarred, stained desktops. Feeble attempts at decoration only emphasized the institutional bleakness: pumpkins and paper cutouts of witches and black cats for Halloween, silhouettes of Pilgrim Fathers and turkeys for Thanksgiving, artificial holly wreaths at Christmas time hung at the windows with their view of a network of neighboring fire escapes, for Easter, lily bulbs that refused to bloom. On Valentine's Day, Miss Robbins's desk displayed a collection of lacy cards, votive offerings from her students that failed to open her heart which remained as tightly shut as the unblossoming lily shoots on the windowsills. Over all there floated that ineradicable amalgam of smells: the persistent chalk dust, varnish and antiseptic. At intervals, a bell, shrill as a fire alarm, resonated through the building, a signal for a mass shift to another location: gymnasium, cafeteria or the yard, where recess released the brute instincts suppressed so long in the classrooms. This asphalt–paved, wire–fenced area resembled a prison court. There all the primary classes were joined and Nicholas and I met again. It was here that I made the discovery that my brother was a butt. Although

I chose the corner farthest from him and pretended not to know him, I could not shut out the scene enacted at recess: Nicholas attacked by a gang of bullies. He put up no resistance but would fall, his long legs sprawling helplessly, while his attackers jeered and danced around his prone body. When they tired of this sport and moved off, Nicholas would rise laboriously to his feet, his abnormal height unsteady and conspicuous among the other children. I can still see his scared white face, the birthmark on his nose now a darker branding of humiliation. He did not cry, nor call for help; he never retaliated, accepting his shame abjectly. Why was he the one chosen? I would ask myself. Was it because he was indefinably "different"? Did his chronic fears, like the scent of an animal pursued, incite the pack? Although I pitied him, I would not go near him; as though his plight might be contagious. Let him not be my brother, I implored some unknown power. Nicholas, however, did have one champion. My tall skinny gangling brother, a Don Quixote, with his own visions, had his Sancho Panza—a short, tough boy, with an oversized head and tousled yellow hair. He would spring to Nicholas's defense with bravura courage and strong fists. Strangely, Nicholas accepted this aid without visible appreciation, intent instead on ingratiating himself with his enemies. My shame mounting, I watched as he distributed money among them. When his supply was exhausted he offered chocolate bars, gold Eversharp pen and pencil and even the empty leather wallet, all of which the tormentors snatched with greed, reserving further torturing for another day. I had been told that these cruelties occurred at other places, whenever the eye of discipline was absent: in the long, dark corridors, the boys' toilet, the locker room. Nicholas often arrived home with empty pockets, but rarely a scratch or a bruise. My awareness of his craven bribes was more horrifying than would have been the sight of any physical wound. Yet as an assimilated, protected child, I was totally ignorant of all Jewish stereotypes: the caricatures of Jewish moneylenders and usurers, the passive ways of ghetto survival. Atavistic memories, like dreams, are buried deep within the subconscious, but despite resistance, they tell us without words, about a buried past, believed to be dead, banished forever from the conscious mind. So, during recess, I cringed away from my own brother, from the flesh and blood of which I, too, was made. And at our school, where various ethnic groups were meant to unite, each day we continued to sing the National Anthem at morning assembly, in praise of our country, the home of us all, the brave.

Illness was the only way of evading school and both Nicholas and I welcomed it. My brother was adept at faking symptoms: heating the thermometer to a suitably alarming degree on a light bulb, overeating more than usual. Greed and purpose usefully combined produced an attack of vomiting that shook with its violence not only the self-made sufferer, but the entire household. But the genuine chest colds, grippes and childhood diseases were plentiful and frightening, each time, to my mother for whom a cough was the discharge of a cannon, a sneeze an exploding bullet, while the thermometer, like a dagger in the heart, caused her pale face to grow paler, the beautiful features ravaged by ill-concealed terror. Fortunately, my mother had two strong bulwarks to stand between her and the menace: at the first danger signal Dr. Elias Steinmetz, our family physician, arrived, followed by Maureen Jones, a trained nurse on call for such emergencies. The doctor was always dressed impeccably, in clerical black with stiff white starched collars and cuffs, and he carried a satchel filled with the occult instruments of his profession. He had snapping jet-black eyes, a high, bald, domed forehead and a small goatee stuck to his chin like a swab of surgical cotton. He was our guru and none of his adoring patients, no member of our family (even my father, who scoffed at all idolatry, human as well as metaphysical) was immune to his hypnotic gaze or resisted his orders delivered in a slow, deliberate, self-confident voice. His word was our law.

"Bed rest—a camomile tea enema—lots of Vichy water—the windows closed at all times—*no drafts.*" . . . "Drafts" were like tornados and only Dr. Steinmetz could save us from the wreckage.

Lacking priest, minister or rabbi, we turned to Dr. Elias Steinmetz who accepted our reverential dependence as his natural right and due. Beneath the touch of his cool dry hand we believed ourselves cured, when he sat on the edge of the bed stethoscope joining his ears to our chests, he was the pilot of our hearts. The penetrating glance of one black eye, the other covered by the moon of his reflector, probed more deeply than X-ray into the secrets of our bodies. "Intuition, a little intuition, goes further in diagnosis than any laboratory machine in the world. Physicians must have faith in their five senses," Dr. Steinmetz would say. By that, one realized that he was referring only to himself, as Elias Steinmetz was notoriously scornful of his medical colleagues, consulting no one else. Now and then, here and there, his "intuition" might lead to the discovery of another doctor (in a different specialty—a surgeon or an ophthalmologist) and he would exclaim, "What hands! with fingers like that who needs brains?"

The other participant in the domestic drama of our illnesses, Maureen Jones, would enter the sick-room with energetic prancing steps, almost a jig, singing in a hoarse voice as she went about her tasks, "Mademoiselle from Armentières," "Parley Voo" or "It's a long way to Tipperary," from World War I. Maureen Jones had nursed the brave soldiers wounded in battle, married one of them who had been severely shell-shocked and was now unable to work. They had a son named Buddy to commemorate their wartime romance. I wondered who watched over him when his mother was taking care of us. But that chapter of Maureen Jones's history was omitted in the version she related to us. She looked like a flapper with her black hair cut short and close to her head, perky points plastered to her prominent, high cheekbones. Her eyes were green and thickly fringed; "St. Patrick's Day eyes," she used to say. She was short and pear-shaped, the upper and lower parts of her body seeming to belong to two different women: her shoulders were narrow, her breasts delicate, but she had broad hips and sturdy legs with thick ankles. Her uniform spanned tautly across her ample buttocks, creasing in vertical lines like bars on sheet music. With her old songs, tales of war heroism and her unquenchable gaiety (sometimes the Irish jig would accelerate into a wild Spanish fandango and she would perch a comb in her black hair at a coquettish angle, kicking her legs so high that her white thighs showed above her garters), Nicholas and I were always sorry to see her leave. Eventually, along with the diseases of childhood, we outgrew the care of Maureen Jones. Later I learned that, despite her sturdiness, buoyancy and unflagging energy, she had, incredibly, died young. I never knew what became of Buddy and the shell-shocked soldier husband.

Nicholas, however, must have needed Maureen Jones more deeply than any of us suspected. One summer, years later, when he lay very ill at a sweltering Italian resort on a scenic, malarial lake far from the supernatural healing powers of Dr. Elias Steinmetz, in passing his hotel bedroom door, I heard him scream in delirium, "Mauress!" (his special name for Maureen Jones). Although the voice belonged to a man, behind it I could detect an infant's call for help in the night.

Today, when I see a flickering, old-fashioned World War I film on television: a hospital scene with bandaged soldiers and valiant nurses, I supply my own sound track: a hoarse, cracked voice singing "Tipperary," and I inhale the vapor of tincture of benzoin from the spout of the tin croop kettle beside the sickbed of my childhood.

The inflexible regimen of convalescence was boring and depressing. Midway between illness and health, a limbo state, we were permitted by Dr. Steinmetz to be "up and around the house . . . away from drafts, of course. . . ." Then, provided there were no "setbacks," we had his blessing to venture outside for ". . . an airing . . . at noon . . . on the sunny side of the street. . . ." Dr. Elias Steinmetz and his cranky remedies have long since gone, but the obedience to his warnings predates him by more than a century and extends beyond the sickroom walls. Caution, moderation, observance of foreign interdictions were precautions practiced by the Jew newly liberated from the ghetto, they remained a tacit motto (source unknown) for us. Just as we trusted the rules of Dr. Elias Steinmetz to keep the enemy, death, at bay; as assimilationists we dared to hope that by conforming we might, gradually, at some future time, attain our goal: the total absorption that would make us indistinguishable from the other citizens of our host nation.

With weak, unused limbs, the convalescent stepped out into the canyon of Park Avenue. At those moments I felt that even an abrupt return to my detested school would have been preferable to this debilitating process; the aimless stroll on the recommended side of the street where every number on the awnings and all the doormen were familiars by force of habit. As Nicholas and I were rarely ill at the same time, I could, however, enjoy an interlude of isolation from him. Just as the churchman of the Middle Ages believed in the Devil and his influence, Dr. Steinmetz feared the contagiousness of germs, and his patient, like one possessed, was segregated until a drop in fever indicated that the Evil One had been exorcised.

Our double tonsillectomy, performed at home, so that even surgery might be tempered by the snugness of domesticity, was an exception. Like Siamese twins, Nicholas and I were joined in dread of the event. My brother, as usual, seized upon the occasion for the acquisition of another costly present. His instinct for barter held firm even through terror.

"I want that hook and ladder big enough to get inside and be pedalled."

"And you, what would you like?" my mother and father asked me.

"Nothing," I lied stoically. For a long time I had coveted a baby doll, a perfectly realistic wax replica that came with a complete layette.

"Come now, Nicholas will have his fire engine. You will be sorry when you have nothing."

But I shook my head, prompted neither by self-denial, courage, nor asceticism. If Nicholas clamored for reward then I would have none. Although we might have tonsils and adenoids in common, and share the pain of their removal, I would use all my willpower to ensure that the similarity would not go further than that.

On the day of the operation, the nursery was shrouded in freshly laundered white sheets, every piece of furniture, each picture on the wall vanished into this sanitized lunar wilderness. Nicholas went first because he was the oldest and then came my turn to breathe the thick, sick-sweet fumes of ether and to be no more. When I awoke from the dead, dazed, retching, my throat on fire, the strange doctors had vanished and Dr. Elias Steinmetz was standing by my bed. I saw him from a great distance, as through the wrong end of a telescope. Black-suited, with his polished dome forehead, pointed white goatee and black X-ray eyes, he was a mythological god, descended to earth in known human form. He spoke in that voice I had heard so often before—slow, deliberate, self-confident.

"When she stops vomiting, give her a few sips of ice-cold milk." The god had uttered and was holding out to me, a mere mortal, the offer of celestial ambrosia.

In the next room Nicholas was screaming like an animal slaughtered. I covered my ears to shut out the helpless blood–curdling sounds.

"Reflected pain," said Dr. Steinmetz referring to my earache: he had returned, now, to his habitual form of omniscient family doctor.

The aftercure following the double tonsillectomy was out of the ordinary, too. The gasoline-saturated atmosphere of Park Avenue would not suffice, and Nicholas and I, with Maureen Jones, were dispatched to Atlantic City for the more vigorous restorative of salt sea air. It was early spring and the ocean was a somber gun-metal gray, the beach deserted. By contrast the boardwalk was thronged: no one listened to the steady warning moan and crash of the waves below. The huge luxury hotels were filled to capacity, the movie palaces, shooting galleries, slot machine arcades, ferris wheel; vendors of every kind hawked their wares, weight lifters, fortune tellers, magicians boasted of their skills to the passing crowd. Nicholas was in his element; his wallet, always replenished by his father, was stuffed, and his hotel room, like a rat's nest, was filled with his purchases and trophies in addition to the railroad schedules, pamphlets, magazines and newspapers that always surrounded him wherever he might be.

The three of us—with Maureen Jones in the middle, to keep peace—rode up and down the boardwalk in an oversized wheel chair. We had our pictures taken in cardboard forests, airplanes, automobiles, our faces peering out of holes in the heads of cardboard bears; we tried all the games and marveled before the jugglers and weight lifters. Through it all, I tried not to notice the invalids' carts threading their way among the rolling chairs and strolling pleasure seekers. Stretcher-like conveyances, they supported prone bodies covered up to their chins. Sometimes a putty face would be jauntily topped by a garish knitted cap. Like the crippled and blind beggars, the unemployed apple sellers among the window shoppers along Fifth Avenue, the moribund went their humble route among the noisy, aggressive fun-hungry crowds on the boardwalk at Atlantic City.

I wanted to walk on the sand by the edge of the sea, but that was considered dangerous, out of bounds. An iron rail divided the games above from the treachery of nature below. It was better to visit the House of Horrors, with its pretend thrills, more prudent than proximity to the rearing, cresting, smashing breakers and their incessant message not meant for human ears. Armed with containers of buttered popcorn, we faced the phony dangers inside the House of Horrors. Maureen Jones squealed dramatically in response to artificial disembodied groans issuing from all sides, the floors rose and fell under our feet, like the deck of an ocean liner in rough weather; we had a bumpy ride in a gondola down a narrow canal between makeshift walls. It terminated in a dump heap of plastic skulls and dismembered plastic limbs, no more disturbing than a demolition junkyard with recognizable remains of what used to be a functioning home. We ran the gamut to the exit flanked by two distorting mirrors. And just as fiery dragons guard a dungeon, a final trial, before the prince in the fairy story is able to reclaim his rightful kingdom, the mirrors at the door of the House of Horrors stood sentinel as we were about to emerge into the light of day. One was to enlarge, the other to diminish; Nicholas chose to stand before the magnifier. In the murky, greenish, convex glass he was turned into a gargoyle: his height was stretched into gigantic width, his features swollen: two caves for nostrils, his lips, grotesque, his eyes pools of greed and fear, his hands, hams with fingers the size of long, grasping arms. More than the caressing speech of the gypsy fortune teller and her crystal ball ("You will have a long life young gentleman—a prosperous one—I see a blond lady . . ."), the distorted image was a prophecy. Although the mirror was mute, it expressed a single word, "excess," and all unknowing in the House of Horrors my brother gazed face to face at the image of his future.

In spite of the bullying and abuse endured by Nicholas at the gloomy institution on the Upper West Side, he was persistently optimistic that his gifts and bribes would ultimately succeed, that he would cease to be the outsider, someone derided. And it was I who dropped out, finding a relaxed haven at a "progressive" school in a small, intimate brownstone not far from home.

When Nicholas reached high school, in conformity with the conventions for boys in our social circle, he was sent to boarding school. Through the intervention of influential friends, he was accepted at Wellington Academy—not at the very top, but High Episcopalian and known for its small quota of Jewish boys. For Nicholas this was considered an honor and a victory and I imagine that he set out on that first day nervously, pride and misgivings mingled.

The campus was traditional British, pseudo-Gothic; classroom and dormitory buildings clustered around the chapel whose slender steeple, visible everywhere, was intended as a constant reminder to the ruffians below of the One who died for them on the Cross. Wellington students gathered twice daily in the chapel. Brushed and scrubbed, in Sunday attire, they dutifully intoned the required hymns, bored, counting the minutes until it would be over. Nicholas learned the words and the music quickly and sang with fervor; he even listened attentively to the sermons delivered by the Reverend Percival Knowlton, hoping that his respectful attention would be honored and that he would, somehow, gain admittance to the coveted Christian paradise. For the other boys the Reverend Percival Knowlton was merely "old windbag," "The Enemy," like all the other masters at Wellington Academy. Morning and evening they squirmed resentfully on the hardwood seats of the chapel. But Nicholas, in secret, looked forward to these solemn sessions; from below, the Reverend Percival Knowlton resembled one of the Gothic saints in the niche of a great cathedral in Europe he had visited with his family. They were outlanders then, and always, but now, he, Nicholas, was allowed to sit right where he was, admiring the elongated living form, the flowing sculptured robes of his own headmaster. Stirred by the tones of the organ and all those young voices joined in praise and supplication, Nicholas, a guest, inside the inner sanctum was raised above his everyday preoccupations in a cloud of unformulated grandiose aspirations.

At other times of the day I could visualize him trooping over the campus, pleased that he was there surrounded by the austere ivy-clad buildings and wide playing fields. He was an ungainly figure, with his exaggerated, unsteady height. Already six feet five, he stooped as though apologizing for this freakishness. His arms and legs, in knee knickers, lacked mutual cooperation so that his progress on the paths was uncertain, as though he were encountering obstacles along the way, when instead the impediments all belonged to his own disjointed body. Just as a tower constructed, too high, with toy blocks wavers, one hoped that Nicholas would reach his destination without tumbling. The "Little Lord Fauntleroy" curls, shorn long ago, had darkened into a wiry unmanageable thatch and when he looked at himself in the mirror, he reviled his large, high-bridged downward–turned nose, badge of his origin, and the ugly stain of the birthmark. His hazel eyes were oddly unchanged from childhood; as with those of a runaway colt's, panic and willfulness could at times disrupt their innocence, giving way to menace and unrestrainable destructiveness. His teeth (inherited from his mother) were his only beauty, an evenly matched set of white ovals as shocking in his pimply adolescent face as a valuable family heirloom—a Dresden china tea service, a lalique vase—in a shabby neglected tenement room.

I was no longer witness, so I cannot say with certainty whether Nicholas needed a Sancho Panza at Wellington Academy, or if he acquired one there. I would guess that the hazing and persecution were even fiercer, but by now my brother was wily in the techniques of passive defense. Furthermore, his ambitions told him that every pursuer halted might be one more step for him toward acculturation, and he was determined to force his way in. At Wellington Academy, Nicholas was divided: one part still prey, while in his dreams he had already joined the hunters. He emulated his classmates as much as possible—sometimes, even lining up against an occasional fellow Jew. Only in his dealings with girls, he did not follow. Nicholas was never shy, his articulate garrulousness was like a rushing torrent, he was uninhibited in any company. But he was oddly prudish, his chivalrous attitude toward the opposite sex excluded him from "dirty talk" in the dormitory and prevented him from sexual experimentation with the conveniently promiscuous "townies." Nor to my knowledge did he ever invite a date to a school dance; he would have been embarrassed to appear with a Jew and he knew almost no one else. He may have invented a fabulous beauty, more satisfying to him than any actual flesh-and-blood adolescent female. His creation could have the blond ethereal perfection of his mother, at other times, she was a dark Spanish señorita with flashing eyes and provocative, audacious gestures.

So I see him at the proms, always on the sidelines, standing by the refreshment table, eating voraciously instead of flirting; indifferent to the teenage dates of his schoolmates, as far from his own imaginings as would be an American assembly line product from one of the sleek expensive limousines in the Thalheim's garage—objects of his childhood lusting.

At home, on holidays, he brought no friend, but he never complained about school. He related at length, with chauvinistic pride, the victories of Wellington Academy at athletic meets. He bragged (un-believably) that he had made the football team. On Parents' Day, the puzzle was solved. Sitting in the bleachers, my mother and father saw that their son was, indeed, connected with the team as the water boy. He brought up the rear, carrying pails too heavy for his long thin, white unmuscular arms. My father, bored with the senseless scrimmage, the piling up of bodies, sat through the game plotting a more fitting position for his son in the future. His heir would be ruler of the small empire of the Meis-tersinger Brewery. As for Nicholas, it is my belief that he felt honored to be serving his athlete-heroes and experienced, perhaps, a bit of their glory, as if the glow from the Grail, was reflected in the humble bucket in his charge. I see him among the helmeted, padded players looking naked and vulnerable in his open sport shirt, sleeves outgrown and loose, baggy trousers. And I hear his cheers, louder, more enthusiastic above all the other voices.

For the senior yearbook, Nicholas was advertis-ing manager. It was his job to go through the town soliciting the local butcher, baker, grocer, phar-macist, etc., insisting on their giving him space in the *Wellingtonian*. His indomitable will was as op-erative among strangers as at home, and he rarely returned to school without the spoils. He also pro-cured for the publication a glossy, full–page ad-vertisement from the Meistersinger Brewery. But just as an American tourist is conspicuous in a Eu-ropean town, the old German script, the trademark of the Bloch enterprise, stood out among the ads of homogeneous New England shopkeepers. And beneath Nicholas's photograph in the yearbook, solemn, with sleeked hair, was the title: *Beer Baron*. Given in the spirit of mockery or respect, I don't know, but it suited both Nicholas and my father who exhibited it to the Bloch clan: a message to announce the latter's intention of placing, in the future, his son upon the throne: chief executive of the Meistersinger Brewery.

I cannot say what my brother learned from books during his time within the ivy-covered pseudo-Etonian halls of Wellington Academy. But it was there, subservient to borrowed British rules and surrounded by the Gentile privileged, that he determined to strangle the Jew within him. Goaded by the suffering caused by his apartness, indoctrinated by his assimilationist family, Nicholas, always an exaggeration, set forth upon his fanatic's endeavor. And, in my mind's eye, I see him, down the years, always wearing his blue blazer, brass-buttoned, with the Wellington Academy crest embroidered in gold thread above his heart.

THREE

THE SUMMER HOLIDAY WAS OVER, IT HAD RESEMBLED all the previous ones. My father, a small, hedonistic general, had led us energetically from city to city, pointing out the sites of interest. We visited every museum, palace and cathedral, dined at every famous restaurant. In deference to my mother's anxiety that urban sightseeing in foreign countries, though educational, did not make for a healthful vacation, we spent a cool gray week near a pebbly beach at a French resort in Normandy, and another, high up, in the pure blue air of the Alps, at a hotel resembling a sanitorium for tuberculars. Although our luggage was plastered with many colorful hotel stickers from the countries we had passed through, this year Germany was missing. ". . . A little trouble . . . unrest," had been reported. But no one took "that fellow, Hitler" seriously, nor his "crazy pronouncements against Jews. . . ." Still it was, perhaps, wiser to be "prudent," and, although there was "nothing to be alarmed about," to avoid Germany for this once.

Now, in the train compartment, I felt as though

I had reached home already. There were our bags securely stowed away in coarse net hammocks, the white antimacassars on the plush seat backs, the same photographs of London Bridge, the Tower of London, St. Paul's Cathedral and Westminster Abby. Our snug quarters were a recurring mobile hyphen that connected, through all the months of travel, one foreign stop to the next. Yes, everything was the same, just as it had always been. And I had no presentiment that it was to be our last trip together. Just as aging is a process of erosion, so slow as to be virtually imperceptible, not preparing any one of us for death in any of its guises, we are equally unaware that our accustomed ways may be interrupted without our volition, our pleasant voyages cancelled. So powerful, so numbing is the masterful narcotic, Habit.

Sitting opposite my mother in the train compartment, I noted, absently, the fine lines on her white skin, but just as I took for granted the Rossetti angel perfection of her face and never thought to exclaim to myself, "How lovely she is!", the appearance of those lines etched by age, like frost patterns on a windowpane, did not cause me to protest, "My mother is growing old!"

The train was moving through the placid English countryside, but we did not notice that the light on the landscape was changing. Travelers, all of us, we know how to read the signs along the route, we take in details: a quaint, thatched–roofed cottage, here, an orderly garden, there, ancient trees, but we are innocents and do not know where we are going. The train plunged into a tunnel with a desperate wail and when it emerged the sky had darkened and light rain was falling. It did nothing, however, to disturb the serenity of the passing scene, spread outside the windows like a plentiful, prim English tea.

Nicholas never looked up from the magazine, *Silver Screen*, in which he was totally absorbed. That summer, along with the rest of the trappings of his luggage—the pamphlets, folders, schedules, newspapers—a collection of movie magazines had been added. It did not seem significant except for the fact that they took up additional space.

"Please throw some of it away," my mother would implore. Nicholas's hotel rooms were disheveled, crowded, and musty with all the papers he amassed. He had forbidden the chambermaids to touch any of it and they were obliged to dust, perfunctorily, around the stacks. "It's not even sanitary," my mother argued as she begged Nicholas again and again.

"No—I refuse to throw anything out. It belongs to me, I bought it all." Nicholas's face grew rigid with that will that rode roughly over the feelings of others.

My mother would appeal to my father. "Please make Nicholas . . ."

But my father was unwilling to spoil by useless arguments his joy in traveling with his family.

"There's no harm in it," he said. And the growing mound of paper accompanied us wherever we went.

I can't remember Nicholas reading a novel: facts,

of every kind, were his nourishment. Nicholas could submit to memory with utmost rapidity the uncorrelated statistics he collected. He could recite the name of every deluxe hotel he had ever stayed at as well as those not yet visited; he knew the hours of arrivals and departures of all the railroads and ocean liners. He retained everything in his cluttered mind: paintings in museums, the dates and events cited at historical places. But they were no more interesting to him than the daily comings and goings at the Gare St. Lazar or Victoria Station. Speed and motion were his drugs, more exhilarating than arrival. But it was, above all, money and the luxuries it purchased that he longed for. Then why was he conserving like a miser those stacks of dated tawdry movie magazines worth only a few cents? Sitting on the red plush banquette, Nicholas was hidden by *Silver Screen*: I examined its cover displaying a colored photograph of a movie star with a toothy smile. But I knew, by memory, my brother's countenance; and although he was now twenty-one, it seemed to be the same face I had been avoiding all my life.

This summer, he had met us in Europe after a year's absence, and it was as though he had never been away. After college, he had been sent to Copenhagen to learn European brewing skills. He lodged with a Danish brewer's family, the same that had extended its hospitality to my uncle (my father's older brother), a generation earlier. This appealed to Nicholas who was a traditionalist and sentimental, especially concerning his Bloch ancestors (from Ludwigsburg to the plant in Brooklyn), a dynasty of brewers that he was about to join. It was the event my father had been plotting since the day his son was born.

While he was away, I gave little thought to my brother, I was too busy with my own life even to feel the relief of his absence. When I attempted to imagine what his days in Copenhagen might have been, the same vision always appeared to me: I saw a lagoon upon which floated a flotilla of swans— all alike, all white, and, in their midst, a black one, my brother. Perhaps in this totally alien atmosphere where he was a true visitor and not a second-class citizen supposed to be like everyone else, but never succeeding, he found some contentment. I see him in the evening healthily tired, after a strenuous day's work at the Copenhagen brewery, enjoying with his hosts a foaming stein of their native brew. Against the icy northern winter they are gathered around a cavernous stone hearth in which the jumping flames are redolent of pine from the nearby forest. In brotherhood, they raise their mugs and lightly touch one against the other, joined by their mutual respect for their craft; like the medieval German guilds that had inspired Wagner's opera and had later brought tears to the eyes of Daniel, the scapegoat of the Bloch clan. Perhaps there were tears in Nicholas's eyes, too. My brother must have been gratified that he, a Jew, an outsider, was so warmly welcomed by this family with their glacier-blue eyes and flaxen hair. Here, perhaps, my brother would be able to enjoy a rare instant of relaxation since he was not forced to glance over his shoulder for a possible tormentor, nor to reach into his pocket with that practiced gesture for the bribe.

Everyone drank together. Nicholas, the outlander, the odd bird, was floating down the lagoon with the white swans.

"Last call, last call!" The lunch gong was growing fainter as it passed down the corridor into the next car.

Nicholas dog-eared a certain page with care and placed the magazine on top of the pile. Reluctantly, he followed us as we lurched like drunkards, thrown from side to side by the momentum of the train, toward the dining car.

Nicholas was back home, but I was at college and saw little of him. He had started to work at the Meistersinger Brewery; and just as an ocean liner too large to make its way into port independently is nosed into its berth by the adroitness of a small tug, Nicholas, propelled by his father, believed he could circumvent the obstacles in his path—the family jealousies and hostilities—until he would arrive at the top. At home, he and my father talked business incessantly, Nicholas expatiating loudly on his extravagant plans for expansion. The solid, old-fashioned Bloch enterprise must be converted, he maintained, into a competitor in the wider world of high finance. Frequently Nicholas's unrelenting vehemence, his eloquence and his agile brain would overpower my father, who would submit to some risky, visionary, costly proposition against his better judgment.

Yet, despite these new involvements, the film
magazines continued to multiply in my brother's
room. One day, driven by curiosity, feeling like a
trespasser, I entered Nicholas's private domain at
the end of the corridor. It was unfamiliar terrain
because, as at Green Meadows, here in our city
apartment, I still found no place for my brother in
my mental blueprint of home. Nor did the room
seem to belong to him, with its walls hung with
English hunting prints (although he had not been
on a horse since that childhood accident long ago),
and banners from Wellington Academy and college
(where he had been a misfit, too), from which he
had commuted to New York, in attendance just
long enough to receive, after four years, his di-
ploma—framed upon his desk.

The magazines (old issues mixed with new) were
everywhere: on his desk, night table, in his closets
and upon bookshelves, many of them torn and frayed
like old papers stacked on a peddler's cart. I selected
one and it fell open, automatically, to a dog-eared
page with a photograph, full-length, of a cool, sleek,
slender, fair actress. She had dainty chiseled features, narrow pale eyes, a small nose, nostrils so
constricted that they looked as though they had
been artificially pinched by the compression of a
clothespin. I picked up another magazine; again it
opened to reveal the same image; another and another, always that face: smiling, pensive, the tough
alley-cat expression in the pale eyes contradicting
the refinement of the rest of her physical person.
"Candida Blanche," I read, "British import who has

set Hollywood on fire . . ." The image did not look incendiary but rather like a frosty glass of ice water among the ripe fruits displayed in the Hollywood marketplace. The puzzle had been solved. My brother had never attached himself to any girl from our small, affluent German Jewish social circle; no one had measured up to his grandiose dreams and, furthermore, he was too insecure to trust a relationship not based upon his money. He had preferred his wildly romantic visions to any reality. And now Nicholas had fallen in love with a photograph!

The next act was soon to follow. Behind the closed door of the living room I listened to the scene. It had the destructive violence of family china being hurled and crashed to bits: my father and Nicholas fighting.

"You're an idiot! It's only a picture, you have never even seen her!"

"I'm going to California to find her and then I will ask her to marry me."

"You don't know what you are saying. Make her your mistress, if you must, but don't talk of marriage. You are crazy!"

My father, who had had relations with actresses before meeting my mother, when he had been forty years old, remained a Victorian in his attitude to sex: certain kinds of women one married, others definitely not. But he usually remained silent on amatory matters. "You people all talk too much," he would say. My mother and I, however, took pride in his former conquests (the facts gathered

here and there from others). Like Desdemona clinging to her general-husband, loving him for his valor
in battle, my father's former exploits among actresses enhanced his attractiveness for my mother,
those "wild oats" sown long ago in his bachelor
years helped to bring the wider, glamorous outside
world into the protected enclosure of her stifling
domesticity.

"I'm willing to stake you to a good time, son,"
my father was saying, "but one doesn't make a wife
of that sort."

"I want her no other way. I refuse to insult her."

"Insult, insult!" my father spluttered. "What do
you suppose her way of life has been before you
clapped your eyes on her photograph in those trashy
magazines? Fortunately, without money in your own
name, she will turn you down. She will laugh at
your ridiculous, naïve proposal. She will show you
up for the fool that you are!"

"That is why you are going to have to help me!"

"Over my dead body . . ."

At this point, Nicholas's screams rose hysterically, his words grew unintelligible. It was the tan-
trum from his childhood when he was fighting for
an expensive new toy. My heart beat painfully; an
old wound reopened. Again I felt my brother's un-
bridled will as a danger, I wanted to run but remained chained to my post, an eavesdropper behind
the closed door. He cannot be my brother—he
can't—I will make it not so, I repeated to myself in
a silent litany that possessed no power to console.

When, at last, father and son emerged, I could

tell by the look of victory in Nicholas's runaway eyes that he had, again, been the winner. My father, by his side, looked shrunken. Common sense, worldly wisdom, humor were defenseless against wild obsession, uncontrollable will and blind romantic innocence.

Opposed by his son, then and always, my father had been denied the freedom to utter one short, single word: No.

I was aware only that my brother was traveling back and forth to California, a grotesque wooer fortified by money in the bank, as earlier, in his school days, he survived with the aid of the stuffed wallet my father could never deny him. I was ignorant of all the details of the courtship: How did Nicholas manage to find Candida Blanche? through a mutual acquaintance, or did he simply force his way into her home or studio? I only knew that he set forth to buy love, humbly asking for nothing in return, neither reciprocity, nor even kindness, always the adorer never aspiring to be the adored. My brother was purchasing merely the right to call that pretty object of his dreams *wife*. The scenes when he was home continued and multiplied. My mother joined the battle, to no avail.

One day, I found her extended on her *chaise longue*, but instead of the welcome I was accustomed to receive, she remained inert, speechless, pale as death. The veins at her white temples were engorged and, just as a parasite weed flourishes and grows tough while the fragile flower in its grip fades and falls, the bulging snake-like veins on my mother's temples seemed to be strangling her diminishing vitality, her life.

Rousing herself at the sight of my shocked expression, not wishing to alarm me, with effort she managed to say, "It's nothing. Just a slight fainting spell—it will soon be over. . . ."

But Dr. Elias Steinmetz had been summoned. He arrived looking virtually unchanged since my childhood. He still wore clerical black, perhaps his pate was a bit more polished, his goatee a shade whiter, but the sparks from his dark leonine eyes were potent as ever. After examining my mother abruptly, he demanded an interview with Nicholas.

Again, through a closed door, I overheard words that filled me with a nameless horror. Dr. Steinmetz was angry, but he did not scream like my father. He remained calm, measured, authoritative. But for the first time I detected a note of cutting sarcasm and scorn in his voice.

"Your mother has a weak heart. Any nervous stress could be fatal to her. I order you to desist, at once, from your foolish venture. Do you understand what I am telling you?"

There was no response from Nicholas, only stunned silence, for once. He could not comprehend: he loved his mother with childlike devotion. It was not possible for him to contemplate her death—she would never abandon him. Always his model of perfection and flawless beauty, goodness and self-sacrifice, she was going to be there for him, forever. His need was so great that he took her presence for granted; she was, for him, eternal, like the seasons, as reliable as the day following upon the night. It was beyond his capacity to believe in a world without her.

Dr. Steinmetz, friend of the family as well as its physician, went on with his stern pronouncements, unbending as commandments. He had no pity for Nicholas, he despised his humility toward women, his prudery. He considered my brother's hysterical outbursts to verge on the psychotic. Among his adoring patients he had the reputation for being a "romantic," a "ladies' man." Despite a slavish wife and daughter to make him comfortable at home, his love affairs were legion. Many a dressing table along Park Avenue and adjacent side streets, where his practice took him, was adorned with his photograph, often in a melancholy pose, head in hands, a faraway look in his somber eyes. Women were attracted to him but he was drawn, most of all (a sign of his distinct double standard for the sexes), to the tempestuous, hysterical type who required his expert help. He despised in Nicholas the very qualities he found so fascinating in the "weaker sex." We had all heard tales of the unfortunate but irresistible "little woman."

". . . and there she stood, the smoking pistol still in her hand, when I arrived . . . her lover lying at her feet . . . luckily it was only a superficial flesh wound . . . but she was half out of her mind, poor little thing . . . and all because of that rotter's faithlessness . . . all for love."

In spite of the highly charged emotional content of these stories, I saw them chiefly in set pictures

—as upon a stage. The scene was a cluttered *belle époque* salon, airless and overfurnished: large ottomans with soft harem pillows, fringed portieres, a filigree bird cage hanging from the ceiling, potted tropical plants, Tiffany glass lamp shades and bibelots covering every inch of space—the heroine, dressed in period costume, cinched waist, bustle, bare shoulders, partly covered by long hair tumbling in disarray. The faithless lover was sprawled on a white bear rug. In my mind's eye, his face is featureless except for a bushy black stage villain's mustache.

"If you are unable to alter your ways, to control yourself and behave like a man," Dr. Steinmetz was saying, "you will have to leave home."

But Nicholas did not leave and the scenes continued. Now I had become mainly impervious to these goings–on; and even the memory of my mother stretched out on her couch, the blue veins marbling her temple and pulsing like danger signals, was growing dim. I was engaged to be married and my preoccupations, at this time, were self-centered. I permitted my mother to exert herself, senselessly, for my wedding preparations. As for Nicholas, he appeared to me across a wide gulch, a gesticulating, mechanically agitated figure, like Punch who supplied the audiences along the Champs Élysées with so much merriment, while leaving me bored, indifferent.

One night, shortly before my wedding, I lay in bed examining each object in the room of my girlhood as though to imprint it forever on my mind before abandoning it for my new life. And just as a traveler boarding a train or boat looks back intently at what he parts from, knowing that every good-bye is a rehearsal for death, I saw with a pang of loss the silhouette of the footboard of my English eighteenth-century mahogany bed, a mountain range, in the semi-darkness, the native land that I would not see again. On my night table the gilded filigree jewel box glimmered faintly. It had belonged to my maternal grandmother and was once filled with the stiff dog collars, jeweled hat pins and ropes of pearls that were part of her wardrobe, which I glimpsed in old photograph albums—a story by Edith Wharton about old New York. Now the coffer contained nothing but my paternal grandfather's heavy gold pocket watch and fob, a pendant of three small enameled white daisies worn by my mother in her girlhood and a few neglected trinkets of my own. These objects lost inside the spacious jewel box were like the caretakers of a deserted *palazzo* that has become a national landmark. Next to it, between bookends, was ranged a set of romances by Alexandre Dumas. Unread for years, their supple forest-green leather bindings were reminders of former birthday celebrations and, somehow, the highly colored adventures of French court life; one after another, strung together like the jewels in the famous necklace of Marie Antoinette, they had become, with the passage of time and their proximity to the coffer, intertwined with my mother's modest daisy chain. I was going to leave them behind, too. The wall cabinet that used to house my collection of miniature animals hung empty and my dressing table, with its ruffled skirt that had made its ritual appearance with the first signs of puberty, would be deserted soon; the three-way looking glass, empty of my face, would be no more than a blank window.

The door opened silently and I saw my mother, another ghostly outline to be outgrown. She was wearing her old shapeless flannel bathrobe, and her hair, released from the heavy bun at the nape of her neck, was braided into a long tail reaching almost to her waist. In the darkness of my bedroom I could not make out the ravages of age and worry on her face, her gray hair looked blond again and she seemed girlish, hesitant, shy.

Heaven forbid! It crossed my mind that this might be one of those traditional mother-daughter talks on the eve of marriage—the facts of life explained between the generations, so embarrassing, as though each new one had reinvented the primal act for itself and was so much the wiser. . . . It would be uncharacteristic for my mother. Timid about many things, her attitude to sex was ahead of her time, even virginity was no shining prize to be presented on the wedding night to the experienced groom. My friends enjoyed talking to her as though she were a slightly older, understanding contemporary. Only I avoided direct intimacy. I was wary of her comprehension, her sympathy—it was too close and might uncover a similarity between us. I appreciated her worth but feared to resemble her, to exist as she did, with that exaggerated empathy for others, that quivering sensitivity, lacking the outer layer of epidermis that protected others from the pain I knew she suffered for their sake.

She sat down on the edge of my bed. "Are you awake?" she inquired softly.

I waited, holding my breath, dreading the trite revelations that would follow.

But her words were not the expected ones. "I just wished to tell you before your marriage, that you and Nicholas. . . ." She hesitated and the silence between us was awkward. "You and Nicholas . . ." she repeated, ". . . need have nothing to do with one another. You do not have to see him again, if he persists in what he is doing. . . . I will not have him ruin your life and your husband's, too."

How could Nicholas possibly spoil my shining new existence? My mother's disclosure was a shock; it was far worse than the embarrassing lesson in anatomy I had been waiting for. It was as though I had never known her. I was still certain that she loved Nicholas, all the more, because of his troubles. Unlike my father, she saw him clearly and felt his pain in her own person, as though it were hers, yet now she seemed to be rejecting him. Were we no longer a family? Although I could not deny that, as far back as I remembered, I had attempted to break the bond that attached me to my brother, yet, somewhere in my subconscious, I had trusted my parents as the guardians of us both. Unlike the embarrassment and disgust my brother had always caused me leading to an imaginery break, my mother's words had a hard finality, and just as a seawall that contains the wild waves may crumble, disintegrate, abandoning four sojourners to isolated perils, my mother was deliberately dispersing the home of my childhood. For my benefit, like a figure in mythology, she was sacrificing her eldest, her only son. But there were no gods to command her. By this act, she was violating the ancient Jewish command of familial loyalty that neither of us had ever studied.

"Don't worry," I lied, "Nicholas can't harm me. I'll be all right."

When my mother leaned down to kiss me before leaving, her lips felt cold, dead, against my hot forehead, but the loose hairs at the end of her braid swung forward, and lightly, playfully caressed my cheek. Suddenly I sat up and hugged her, our roles reversed. With sadness, I assumed the load of a mother's heart, and, for an instant, my only wish was to protect her against her own vulnerability. To what? That night, I could find no answer.

Now, a lifetime removed, my mother dead for over forty years, my father, my brother gone also, I begin to understand. My mother—like all assimilated Jews—carried a permanent heavy burden of general insecurity and fear. Nicholas, with his outrageously unconventional behavior, in public view, might inflame the social ostracism we dreaded. He might hinder (my mother believed) my progress out of the past into a future—perhaps my children's or my children's children's—where Jewishness would no longer exist, its perils and banishments, no more than someone else's nightmare. To this end my mother had been willing to deny her natural instincts. Intelligent, loving, gentle, sensitive, she was telling me on the eve of marriage to renounce family—as it was given me—my birthright. And for this purpose, like a surgeon, she had taken the knife into her delicate hand to excise her son, my brother, out of my existence.

The day arrived, at last. Nicholas returned from California with his prize. When he introduced me to Candida Blanche, I felt we had already met, so like her photographs was this animated, tangible presence in our home. From the movie magazines I recognized the dainty, ladylike appearance in which only the shrewd expression in her narrow feline eyes hinted at something grasping. She was dressed all in pearl-gray and both her British accent and her wrist-length white kid gloves struck me as theatrical properties. Nicholas was beaming. Although his beloved was several years older than he and vastly more experienced, he seemed more a proud parent than a suitor. Despite my minute observation of Candida Blanche, I was able to note that Nicholas was wearing his blue Wellington Academy blazer with the golden escutcheon embroidered over his heart.

"This is Candy," he said, sounding prematurely possessive. He appeared more poised and confident than I had ever seen him before and secure in the belief that my father and mother would receive his fiancée with open arms—as bewitched at the sight of her as he had been.

Everyone behaved with circumspection, but I felt

a trap had been laid. It seemed connected, in some way, with the polished formal silver tea service in readiness in the living room. The ornate urn, architectural as a great cathedral, with the subservient creamer and sugar bowl below, like a huddled village, were heirlooms from my maternal grandmother. Beneath the kettle, the sterno fire was as ritualistic as the one inside the dead soldiers' monument under the Arc de Triumphe. The tea caddy, which I used to play with as a child, was like a tourist's souvenir of St. Peter's, a tiny replica of the large urn. All of it—even the cinnamon toast on the gold-rimmed plate, seemed to be saying, Look at us, we represent tradition, gentility, you are not one of us. She and we were competing actors, face to face: rivalry, resentment, hatred, masked by the ceremony of afternoon tea, the real thing concealed behind the bivouac of good manners.

I never learned the denouement, but soon after that meeting Candida Blanche returned to Hollywood and the whole affair ended. I imagine the financial terms were unsatisfactory. My brother's bragging had probably exaggerated his wealth and the sum his father would consent to give him. At any rate, the worshipful suitor was jilted; but strange to say, after such a lengthy tenacious passion, my brother's recovery was surprisingly rapid. It reminded me of the time in our childhood, at Green Meadows, when he had clung, sobbing, to the cocker spaniel puppy, Merry, and then had forgotten him quickly in the excitement of a new electric train. Now, to my father's relief and joy, the brewery engaged all Nicholas's enthusiasm, and it was as though Candida Blanche had never existed. The collection of movie magazines disappeared with her. Yet, just as when a painter makes portraits of different models, no matter how much they may vary in the flesh they are all related on canvas through the personal vision of the artist's eye, in a later obsession of Nicholas it was possible to recognize the pattern, the indelible outline of his first unrealized love.

PART 2

REFLECTIONS IN A DISTORTING MIRROR

ONE

After a day at the brewery I pictured you returning to your house in Westchester County. Its name, High Hill, like all things connected with you, was a magnification. Your terrain could boast of no greater elevation than a steep entrance driveway leading to the front door, crowned by its glass fantail. Along with the Georgian facade, the forest green shutters, walled garden, it bore a certain resemblance to Green Meadows, our first childhood home. But it was disturbingly different also, like a familiar place revisited in a dream.

Laboriously, you climbed the graceful double-arched stairway, your heavy iron leg braces (they had appeared six years earlier, to correct your short tendons) clanked like a robot on every step. Did the window bench remind you, Nicholas, of that other perch, long gone, my preempted territory, from which you, especially, were excluded?

"Little Miss Margo, Little Miss Margo, are you there?" you called.

But your wife, seated before the mirror of her dressing table in her bedroom, made no response.

She was carefully plucking the already pencil-thin, immaculate lines of her eyebrows. Her hair was teased into a modish "bird's nest," her expertly painted, shapely lips were set and determined. Yet her sullen, discontented expression could not mar the flower loveliness of her face.

"Miss Margo, your Bow-Wow is home!" you shouted again.

Margo Duke, now Mrs. Nicholas Bloch, rose silently and shut her door, and you continued your solitary way to your room.

There your masseur awaited you. He greeted you with ceremonious enthusiasm, his master, as so much length of unresisting putty given over to the skilled hands of his métier.

Two years before, I had met your bride, following your secret marriage in Maryland. In the elevator rising to your honeymoon suite in the Waldorf Towers, our father appeared, as nervous as a Hasidic groom about to see his betrothed for the first time beneath the wedding canopy. What was he about to find?

Margo Duke was a successful high-fashion photographer's model—more than that, we did not know. Her delicate features, her slender, neat, small-boned, sophisticated image, were familiar from the glossy pages and the covers of *Vogue* and *Harper's Bazaar*. Her type is rare today, displaced by the interestingly asymmetrical face, the athletic androgynous body.

"Well, what do you think of my Little Miss Margo? Do you approve?" you asked in high good spirits.

And all through that evening, you carried on a monologue, extolling your wife. You were oblivious to her impassive silence.

"Isn't she beautiful?" you went on. "Wait until you meet her son, Sebastian—he's always called Duke by everyone—he's ten years old. I have already bought a house in the country, with a swimming pool for him, a tennis court, and I am going to get him a puppy and a kitten—"

At the mention of her son, Margo's black eyes, hard and glittering as the gem on her finger, melted into human warmth. But it was your incessant chatter, Nicholas, that saved the occasion. I examined my new sister-in-law: her sleekness, her refined manner: she had a small, chiseled nose (reminding me of your first love, Candida Blanche), a heart-shaped face with a firm, rounded, cleft chin, ears like tiny rosy shells, and perfect red lips, forbiddingly shut, her smile was rare. Despite her fashionable clothes, her sophisticated veneer, she looked prim, like a small-town schoolteacher from her native Kansas.

Our father's customary urbanity, his appreciation of beautiful women, were subdued by unhappy doubts concerning your precipitous marriage. Adversaries, he and Margo exchanged glances of suppressed hostility and suspicion.

But you, the exuberant groom, remained impervious to these discordant currents, as you talked on and on, elated by this latest possession—as always you had grown larger, more self-assured, through your purchases.

You were especially proud of your oval dining room at High Hill, with its pearl-gray walls, like the interior of an oyster shell. Your table was set with the cut crystal and English china that had belonged to our mother. Our father, as a bachelor-widower, dined out often, and I, unsentimental, different from you, had no wish for heirlooms— melancholy reminders of our mother's death surviving her, the relics of a childhood that I hoped I had outgrown. Though your youth had not been happy, you clung to its remains, while my home bore no trace of the past. When you spoke of our mother and reminisced, there were tears in your eyes and your voice choked. I cringed from your facile sentimentality, I would bear my loss in silence.

So, following a day at the brewery, it fell to you to dine with your new wife and son at a table in replica of an earlier generation. The practical plastic mats of contemporary suburban life were not for you and you addressed Margo across your mother's white damask tablecloth.

"No, not that way—this is the way we used to do it"—or, "We always had finger bowls and fruit or flowers on the center of the table—"

Your lessons were not intended as criticism; rather, they were an attempt to merge two beloved women —your mother and your wife, for you, alike in beauty, purity, perfection: a single goddess to be worshipped but never attained.

But for Margo those good-natured directives were barbs, reminders of early deprivations. And they made her feel inferior—not to her husband, but to a nameless order of things that had not been her birthright. And just as a self-educated person may discount his learning and envy the force-fed dunce who has passed through the stately halls of an Ivy League college, Margo, her career abandoned, exposed to your domestic instructions, turned bitter inside the home which she would never feel was hers.

"Darling pussycat, you must ring the bell for the waitress—"

Your wife would comply with a shrug of her sharp shoulders, pretending that these foolish things were matters of indifference to her, while each day in her luxurious prison was destined to stretch out into an eternity of boredom and unself-respecting idleness.

Only when she considered her son did the misery seem worthwhile. After all, she had done this for him and he was everything to her. Thanks to her marriage, there would be no more strained, unsatisfactory visits to that boarding school for young children of single, working parents, no more brief weekends together in her cramped New York City flat, no more exhaustion under glaring lights in photographers' studios to provide for her child and herself an unsatisfactory existence. She had taken some pleasure in her success and in her independence, but it would do no longer. A feminist by instinct, if not by credo, she had left Duke's father, a Depression victim, soon after their son had been born, determined to make it alone. But, when you appeared, Nicholas, holding out a dream life for Duke, Margo could not resist. . . . And now, there was the tennis court, the swimming pool, the expensive day school, and, most important, you had legally adopted your stepson. He would be your heir, as if he were your own flesh and blood.

"But he must keep his own name," you insisted.

You would not inflict upon him your Jewishness; furthermore, Sebastian Duke had a noble ring.

The Irish waitress in her black uniform and frilly white apron (a reincarnation of the Bridgets, Delias, Kathleens of our childhood) appeared with the dessert.

Beneath the table Duke's scuffed sneakers moved restlessly as he counted the minutes until his release, when he could join his friends in a ball game or a gathering at the neighborhood drugstore.

Like his mother, Duke was small-boned, well-made; he had the same chiseled nose, round cleft chin, thickly fringed eyes. You admired his beauty, Nicholas, second only to his mother's, but right now you were concentrating on your food, your head almost touching your plate, in your haste and greed, as though the sweet might escape the eagerness of your hungry mouth. You were blissfully unaware of the disgusted glances directed at you by two pairs of thickly fringed stony eyes: onyx black and granite gray.

At the back of your house there was a brick terrace, white-balustraded, shaded from the summer sun by a blue-and-white striped awning. You had built a shallow flight of steps down to the swimming pool, where the aquamarine water was alive with tanned, splashing young limbs: Duke and his friends at play—laughing, shouting, flying through the air from the diving board, creating miniature waves in the pool with the dolphin-swoopings of their never ceasing activity.

"Duke is by far the best swimmer and diver," you would brag.

Your boastings about your stepson were perpetual; Margo remained impassive. But when you asked a guest at your home, "Isn't Little Miss Margo beautiful? Doesn't she remind you of Vivien Leigh?" that contemptuous look would return to your wife's black eyes.

Margo, like a dowager leafing through an album of pictures of her youth, still poured over her professional photographs with nostalgic pride, but she resisted her husband's lavish compliments with steely distaste.

She sat erect and controlled under the striped awning that protected her flawless white skin from the sun. Her beauty was useless now, no longer the sole support of her child; yet, just as a hired gardener works conscientiously, expertly on a plot of land not his own, Margo, detached from her own pulchritude, continued to tend it as carefully as before. For what reason, for what person, she did not know. She repulsed her husband's attentions, and the admiration of other men was even more distasteful to her. She had always scorned masculine advances; she would be no plaything for their arrogant lust.

How often I had heard the words that made me cringe in shame at my blood bond with you, my brother. "At least Nicholas is different. He is not like other men, he is humble," Margo would say.

"Duke has forgotten his snorkel in the house. I'll get it for him," you might remark.

Even more cautiously than usual, because you had left off your leg braces, clinging to the railing for support, you descended the shallow steps. Dressed in your weekend playclothes—Bermuda shorts and bright-colored polo shirt, you were a grotesque tragicomic figure. Your long thin legs, narrow as a stork's, were unstable support for your towering height. Holding out the snorkel like a propitiatory gift, you approached your stepson and his agile companions. It had all happened before. You were the water boy who had once carried the pails with deference to the team at Wellington School. Then, as now, you felt no envy of the others' dexterity. Rejoicing to be of service, you basked, vicariously, in the glory of the young athletes. . . .

TWO

Does one ever actually know another human being? Those nearest to us are constructed from habit and the temperature of our emotions. They are mere appendages to ourselves, blurred, lacking in contour. After they are dead, we seek to bring them back, but memory presents us with disconnected pictures, a patchwork quilt, and out of its haphazard pattern we try, in vain, to make order, to recreate the person we have lost and, alas, have never known.

Among the scenes with my father, I find one which presents him seated at an old-fashioned, homely double rolltop desk in his office at the brewery. It is the same desk that had been used by *his* father and his grandfather before him. Opposite him sits his brother (two years his elder), my Uncle Charles. Joined by the ancestral double desk, they are like twins, despite their physical dissimilarities and their personalities, even more disparate. Uncle Charles is mild-faced, his beard resembles our grandfather's, but it is sparser, less snowy. It has a sandy hue and his eyes are watery blue. He has retained the Teutonic manner of his father, but he is gentler, more friendly.

"How is Daddy's little girl today?" he would ask me, pinching my cheek. I did not altogether trust his geniality. Of his deep feeling for my father, however, I was certain. He had amply demonstrated this when, after running the brewery all his life—surviving Prohibition and the Depression years—he stepped down when my father quit his engineering career to take the reins of the family business into his own hands. Both of them well past middle age, Charles became chief of the brewing department, and our father assumed the responsibilities of president.

"Mr. Charles" and "Mr. Henry" were beloved by their employees. Charles, slow, deliberate, patient, prematurely venerable, and Father, quick, impatient, clever, humorous—one fair, the other swarthy, with a black tonsure barely tinged by gray. At the lunch table in the "old house" where the brothers had been brought up, they are the hosts. "Mr. Charles" still has his place at the head, and he is a reassuring sight—a sign of continuity—as he wipes his sandy beard with an oversized linen napkin after sampling the latest product—in a classic gesture indigenous to brew masters through the centuries. It is he who guards tradition: he has never left Brooklyn and lives with his wife (the daughter of an Aryan German-American brewer), and his children in a commodious house overlooking Prospect Park.

"Mr. Henry" brings a breath from the world outside with him. His well-tailored suits, Sulka shirts, Charvet ties proclaim him not only a New Yorker, but a habitual cosmopolitan traveler, too. Yet he has not abandoned his beginnings, he feels at home in the "old house" and relishes the hare stew and heavy German dumplings prepared by the brewery cook, as much as the most subtle cuisine to be found in any expensive French restaurant. Our mother, appreciative of his loyalty to his past and to the family enterprise, had lovingly nicknamed him "Bush," after the Bushwick section where the plant was located. The area might be a slum, sordid beyond the brewery gates, but everyone was proud of Meistersinger, which had endured for amost a century at the same site. True, the Bloch clan had not made the meteoric rise from peddler to merchant prince, as many in their German-Jewish circle had done. But there was something comfortable about more modest riches that had originated in Bavaria prior to the 1848 arrival in the United States. And, in addition, it was felt that the manufacture of beer was preferable to dry goods—it sounded somehow more German, less Jewish.

With your entrance into the brewery, Nicholas, the atmosphere grew tense. The cousins in the business protested your position as advertising director. Because of your father's maneuverings, you, a newcomer, had supplanted an older man who was first demoted, then eventually disappeared altogether. And Uncle Charles, who had shown no opposition to the takeover of his younger brother, did he already visualize you as heir apparent? Were you a scapegoat for him, the outlet for suppressed envy? Although the brothers continued to sit, like Tweedledee and Tweedledum, companionably facing one another at their double rolltop desk, one could see resentment in Uncle Charles's watery blue eyes. Like a shadow cast over a still pond, presaging a change in the weather, it disturbed the peaceful landscape of fraternal love.

The office of the director of advertising at the Meistersinger Brewery—your place of work, Nicholas —was next door to the room where your father and uncle sat at their old-fashioned double rolltop desk in the worn, musty atmosphere of age. Your office, by contrast, was a marvel of chrome, Lucite and glass brick, a Madison Avenue enclave, buried in the back streets of Brooklyn. At your desk of Napoleonic size, you spent hours on the telephone with the agency, plotting more and more costly methods for publicity. There were few personal touches in your office, but after your marriage, the photographs of Margo and Duke confronted you during your work day. Your wife appeared aloof and grave, but Duke was grinning widely in lurid color by the agency's foremost photographer. In his ten-year-old face, Duke's teeth showed too large, and each freckle was reproduced faithfully in its true dimension. At the back of his tousled head he wore a Yankee cap, and in his arms he hugged his pet spaniel, Carmencita, grandly named by you for Francisco Franco's only daughter. I knew of your admiration for the Spanish dictator, but I ignored it, as I did all your vociferous, misguided enthusiasms. Only much later, it appeared grotesque and I asked myself how you, a Jew, could identify yourself with a cause backed by Hitler and Mussolini. And the answer, I found, is that it was precisely this Jewishness and your repudiation of it that drove you, consciously or subconsciously, to support General Franco during the Civil War. Just as a hunted animal relies on its camouflage, blending in with its surroundings to save itself from attack, you trusted that your identity would be blurred in the midst of Christians in a cause in which no other Jew was likely to be found. Although you stood alone in this, it seems to me now that we, your family although opposed to Hitler, would remain, for the most part, shamefully silent about the Holocaust itself.

When the United States entered the war, you were again apart from the others. Before 1941 you had been an America Firster, and after Pearl Harbor you were classified physically unfit for active service. While other young men rushed into uniform, you donned those iron leg braces that I can still hear clanking through the years, a ghostly accompaniment to the theatre of your life that I am reproducing in the alternate light and shadow of memory.

So you stayed at your post at the brewery, using your relentless energy to force your father into effecting the costly changes you fought for. And just as a racing driver, who, having won every contest, must increase his speed ever more recklessly until the final crash, you followed your victories with greater and riskier demands. I picture you before your marriage, still living at home in the large apartment punctuated by empty rooms, like a mouth with missing teeth. Father slept in his "dressing room," next to Mother's unused bedroom, where all remained intact, unchanged—objects surviving without her.

You used the early mornings to argue with Father about business. Through the closed door of his bathroom, he could be heard wallowing in his tub like a playful walrus. But you had never been deterred by obstacles to your will. You stood behind the door and screamed, "If we don't go forward, we will go backward!" You were insisting on the purchase of another brewery on the West Coast.

Your father, in answer, could still be heard snorting in the water, enjoying the pleasures of the bath despite your barrage. At last he emerged, his body entirely enveloped in a large towel, only his tonsured head showing, his hair ruffled and curling from the steam, his brown-pink skin glowing with health. Wrapped in the bath sheet, he was now a Roman senator holding out against barbarian invasion. But by the time he was fully dressed for business—the old-time ankle-length long john underwear, worn in all seasons, the three-piece suit, vest bisected by gold watch chain, foulard bow tie beneath the chin, white handkerchief cresting jacket pocket—his own control had given way, his temper released, he hurled at you: "You are an idiot! If I listened to you, if we go national, we will be ruined!"

The fight went on during breakfast, the news in the morning newspapers could not stem the tide. Father's pleasant morning ritual, a luxurious bauble, was splintered. But as the battle raged, gathering momentum on both sides, did Father already know who the victor would be—who the vanquished?

At the brewery, you often crossed the threshold, the frontier dividing your metal-and-Lucite kingdom from the shabby, oak-and-brown-leather domain of your father and uncle. The latter maintained a hostile silence in your presence. But Father, before his brother, never opposed your demands; he could only look up at the six-foot-six giant of his own begetting—and capitulate.

You had already effected many minor changes: the bottle labels that had proclaimed the family product in gilded archaic German script were replaced by smart modern scarlet-and-black lettering, the bottles themselves had been redesigned and (in the view of the old guard) unappetizing cans had made their appearance on grocery shelves. The sturdy yellow delivery trucks, as familiar on the streets of New York as the corner lamppost or the mailbox, were scrapped for a new model and had become obsolete like the brewery horse and wagon of the nineteenth century. But small things could never satisfy your voracious appetite for spending, and you continued to press for the California brewery, entering into negotiations without the consent of your seniors.

Reaction against you rose—your family became your enemy, the board of directors plotting your overthrow. Again and again, your father warned you of your danger. But you did not believe in it. Amiable, affectionate and trusting, when not actually prevented from having your way, you would answer, "But they are good friends. They will agree that I am right."

And you followed your unwary, headstrong course.

The time had come for Father to act.

It was spring of 1939, and the World's Fair spread over the swampland of Flushing Meadow like an overgrown amusement park. The crowd flocked, eager for this synthetic travel, confined to the backyard of New York City. As one approached, the Trylon and Perisphere logos—symbols—welcomed the tourists.

Father had chartered a yacht for the day. It was a poor imitation of the cruisings of his former bachelor parties, just as his companion of the moment, a pretty, pallid blonde (many years his junior), was no substitute for his dead wife. But his zest for living remained strong, and just as a gourmet may turn gourmand, he was able to enjoy the rented ship and the inadequate female copy languidly stretched out on a deck chair by his side. Nicholas, you were leaning over the rail, awaiting someone who had not yet arrived. You wore your blue blazer with the Wellington School escutcheon embroidered in gold thread over your heart, a garment that always signified, for you, an important occasion. The guest of honor on this outing was to be Armand de la Riviere, a French multimillionaire entrepreneur whose holdings all over the world included many breweries.

I never knew how or where Father had met him, but I had heard him mention the name, referring to de la Riviere as a "swell"—a word I detested because it seemed to cast an uncharacteristic humility over my father. Now I realize that on the contrary, that designation, on the lips of a bon vivant, was stimulating, tangy, a blend of many ingredients he savored—cosmopolitanism, old wealth, connoisseurship and, of course, the good fortune not to have been born a Jew.

Armand de la Riviere was mounting the gangplank followed by his son, René, and Dr. Helmuth Schneider, de la Riviere's advisor on technical matters concerning the brewing industry. Amalia and Ursula Schneider, his wife and daughter, brought up the rear.

Imagination is often a highly colored pre-form that drains form itself, so that when we encounter reality we stand before it disappointed at its insignificance. In our childhood, in the hothouse atmosphere of a French resort hotel dining room, the headwaiter had pointed out to us the Prince of Wales at a nearby table. I followed the guiding glance and saw a yellow-haired young man in golfing tweeds, unremarkable among the other guests at the hotel. I thought the headwaiter, with his dignified mien, formal dress, striped waistcoat spanning his ample stomach, more royal. The king-to-be continued his lunch, unconcerned that in the eyes of one person inside the dining hall of the Hermitage Hotel, he had already toppled from his hereditary golden throne. Now I observed Armand de la Riviere and experienced a similar surprise. Where was the worldly aristocrat? In his stead, I beheld a slight person, with close-set anxious eyes and a twitching nose which reminded me of the distracted rabbit in *Alice in Wonderland*.

As he stepped onto the deck, he and my father shook hands with the ceremonious cordiality of admirals about to conclude a victory at sea. This pantomime was puzzling, because, as far as I knew, this was to be no more than a pleasant day of sightseeing for the benefit of the foreign visitors, ending at the Bavarian Pavilion, where the Meistersinger Brewery had recreated from old pictures a replica of the original Ludwigsburg beer garden on Long Island soil. In view of this it was odd, also, that with the exception of Uncle Charles accompanied by his wife, no family executives from the brewery had been invited.

While Father and Armand de la Riviere conferred, you, Nicholas, escorted René on an inspection tour of the borrowed yacht—proudly—as though it had actually belonged to you. René, younger than you (not yet twenty), was sleek and handsome. He laughed easily, revealing teeth gleaming in his dusky Latin face. I am certain that he pretended polite interest, but his concentration must have wavered, he had known many such vessels and more splendid ones. When you described your advertising schemes for the brewery, your determination to purchase a West Coast plant, René suppressed a yawn and exclaimed, "Everyone in the United States thinks only of business. In Europe we know how to play. My father wants me to study economics at Harvard University, but I don't want to. I ski, play polo, I enjoy myself with the girls. I don't understand—always work, work, work in this country!"

And René attempted to adjust his light-footed step to your clumsy uncertain gait, looking up at you, as you talked without cease, while you stooped in an effort to bring yourself closer to him.

The Schneiders remained slightly apart. As refugees from Munich, only recently arrived in the United States, their English was not of the best. They were roly-poly and overdressed, the ladies' hair, elaborately coiffed, still smelled of the beauty parlor. All three had identical heavy blue eyes and the same melancholy expression, as though marked more surely by exile than by consanguinity. Dr. Schneider rubbed his doll-size hands together with bonhomie or, perhaps, nervousness. Upon being introduced, he bowed so obsequiously that it seemed as though his flesh might split like the tight casing of a German sausage.

Everyone was now aboard, the captain pulled up anchor, and we started our leisurely cruise on Long Island Sound, hugging the shore where exhibition buildings from all the nations advertised their wares as in a marketplace. Multicolored flags flapped cheerfully in the gentle spring breeze that smelled of salt from the marshes. But from time to time, there arose also a foul odor of sulphur, sickening as rot. The sights were gaudy and dissociated: fake windmills from Holland, rococo Italian *palazzi*, streamlined glass structures were neighbors to Swiss chalets and cobbled medieval streets led to abstract sculpture gardens and minarets. Nicholas, you lingered longest and most lovingly at the automobile displays; the deluxe foreign models your favorites. You stroked their shining hoods, their sleek bodies with the sensuous pleasure that I imagined your prudishness must have denied you with women. Side by side, all the exhibitions were shown in friendly competition, but technocracy and commerce reigned: twin gods promising the avid viewers a heaven of Progress, an alternative salvation.

At dusk we disembarked at the Bavarian Pavilion, where we took place of honor at the imitation Ludwigsburg beer garden. True, there were no linden trees to shed their pods upon the checked table cloths, no military in scarlet and gold to sing their comradely garrison songs; but the place was gratifyingly filled to capacity with tourists. Waitresses were in authentic peasant dirndls and the beer foamed in stone mugs imported from the drinking cellars of Munich.

Father seated his guests, placing Armand de la Riviere near enough so that they might continue their conversation in snatches. Most of it consisted of dull business generalizations, but occasionally Armand would interject his more personal worries concerning the burden of his colossal fortune. And then, his facial tic accelerated so that his pince-nez jiggled on the bridge of his sharp nose like mirrors trembling in an earthquake.

"I thought it safest to convert a portion of my assets into gold brick," he said, in his cultivated accent with its unidentifiable hint of foreignness. "I have buried it in what I pray will prove to be an impregnable hiding place."

I had a vision of the golden piles concealed beneath the ground like in-grown pyramids. But by no stretch of the imagination was it possible to endow Armand de la Riviere with the royal aspect of a pharaoh. Like the White Rabbit, he nervously consulted his watch and glanced toward the door —"Oh, dear, oh, dear," he might have been murmuring to himself, "I shall be late"—and his troubled countenance registered confusion. What important event had been forgotten, what engagement elsewhere was awaiting his arrival? Where was that rabbit hole? Would it lead him to the buried site of his precious hoard?

Father stood up and raised his mug to toast the guest of honor and then to salute the young heirs, Nicholas and René.

"To the future and the hope of a partnership that will join Armand de la Riviere, his family and his associates from across the sea to the Meistersinger Brewery. May we be united, in friendship and prosperity, working together in harmony from generation to generation."

When he resumed his seat, I thought I detected tears in my father's eyes. I had never seen him cry before.

Armand de la Riviere acknowledged the toast with polite thanks. I waited in trepidation for you to begin one of your long embarrassing speeches combining boastfulness and subservience. But, to my relief, you remained silent. Perhaps you considered the perfection of the setting you had created, here at the Bavarian Pavilion, more eloquent than words. Or was it that your sentimental feelings had carried you backward in time? The facsimile beer garden merged with the original one in Ludwigsburg and you were no longer Nicholas Bloch, son of Henry, son of Karl. You were Joseph Bloch, the founder, your great-grandfather. You sat in your beer garden that flourished in a cozy hierarchical society, the king, the church, the garrison, your brewery and the peasants in the fields—all in place. Secure in your niche, there was no mobility upward or downward, and the meaty smell of malt satisfied you and told you who you were, an industrious, thriving German burgher.

Family legend has it that the emigration to America was due to Joseph's well-known liberal views. After the failure of the revolutions of 1848, the prosperous brewer, disillusioned and uncertain about the future of a business whose owner's ideas were in disharmony with prevailing politics, decided to emigrate with his entire family—including brothers, sisters, in-laws and their numerous offspring, eighteen in all. His descendants in Brooklyn shared a mental picture of him being carried on the shoulders of his loyal workmen, in a triumphant march out of town toward the New World. In this myth, handed down through three generations, the words "ghetto," "Diaspora," "pogrom" were never uttered. They belonged to the vocabulary of another people. Ardent assimilationists, the Blochs had torn out the pages of the book of Jewish history. It was as though we had originated all at once in the nineteenth century with Joseph. As a child, I had a vision of him, looking as he appeared in his portrait in the brewery lunchroom, stern-faced, dressed in a stiff-winged collar and black suit, plummeted from the sky into a trellised beer garden, shaded by linden trees, where the soldiers in scarlet-and-gold uniforms sang lustily as they drank the brew. He, the primal begetter, would provide. . . . Nicholas, in your ersatz garden, did you find surcease from insecurities and fears in your dreams?

René de la Riviere did not speak, either. He would have preferred to have been at his club in Paris, mounted on his polo pony swinging his mallet with easy skill—rather than to be seated at the Bavarian Pavilion toasting strangers in beer from chunky, heavy mugs.

Dr. Helmuth Schneider rose. "As the lowly representative of the illustrious Armand de la Riviere, I too trust that a partnership will be sealed, in the near future. In which event I shall perform my duties as ambassador to the esteemed firm of the family Bloch to the best of my abilities."

"Prosit," said my father.

"Prosit," echoed the others.

Only Uncle Charles looked troubled. Like an oracle, he seemed to be seeing into a disturbed future for his beloved brewery.

And at this distance in time I, too, realize that just as a microbe contracted in a foreign land may lie dormant only to erupt, later, into a fatal illness, this convivial dinner to introduce the de la Rivieres contained the poison that was destined eventually to extinguish altogether the century old Meistersinger Brewery, the pride of the family.

When the party left the Bavarian Pavilion, it was night. The Trylon pointed its long portentous finger into a black sky. But the warning went unheeded. The holiday seekers played until a late hour and the fair was bright, illuminated by artificial lights as splendid as the explosion of the final rocket at a Fourth of July celebration. We boarded the yacht, homeward bound. The make-believe cruise was ended.

There are certain events that with the passage of time assume the unnatural color, the improbable outline of fantasies conjured up in a fever. As I continue to reconstruct your history, Nicholas, I come across one of those real/unreal incidents. It had been the high point of your career, but I can no longer recall the reason for my participation in it. Despite my efforts to the contrary, it appears that I remained part of your life, just as you were part of mine.

I see you there, larger than human, seated in a captain's chair in the harsh metallic sun of a winter's day in Palm Beach. The year is 1948 and the first Miss Meistersinger is being photographed, a Venus arisen from the sea of your imagination on the hard shell of a publicity agent's office. She was to make you and the brewery known throughout the nation's growing lobby of advertisers. As though your new position required a corresponding increase, you had grown to colossal stoutness, your ponderous presence presided over the crowd surrounding you. Your father, dwarfed and tentatively proud, stood in the background; there were photographers, their crew, advertising "idea" men, "artists," executives from the brewery and family board members, rendered an impotent minority with the advent of the de la Rivieres. Again Father had succeeded in persuading his brother, Uncle Charles, into agreement and they had turned over much of their voting stock to the foreigners in order to ensure the security of your position at the brewery. But, installed on your Hollywood director's throne, the creator of Miss Meistersinger, there was no one, including your enemies, who did not regard you with respect. And, just as a pacifist bystander is moved, in spite of himself, by martial music and the parading of soldiers, I, your reluctant sister, experienced a surge of pride at your new success. You were always a creature of extremes: once a pathetic butt, now, in the tinsel glory of your promoter's coronation, a king.

I searched for the congenital birthmark on the high bridge of your nose. You had attempted to have it removed more than once, but it always returned, a stubborn emblem of your insecurity, humiliation and fear. In the dazzling light of the sun and the photographer's tinfoil reflector screens, it had vanished. But I could still detect the spot where it had been: the shadow of a shadow remained.

Jill Boyd, duly elected by the public as the first

Miss Meistersinger, the winner picked from among hundreds of candidates, was posing on the grounds of the Palm Beach luxury resort hotel. She was wearing a full-skirted summer dress and a cherry-red, wide-brimmed straw hat. Beneath it, her shoulder-length chestnut hair showed, artfully disarranged, as though blown by a gentle breeze. A natural type, "the girl next door," she had golden skin, a tall, long-limbed, athletic body that radiated health and outdoor living. She remained patiently, arrested in action, a watering can poised in mid-air. Her smile was unwavering, and for hours she showed no signs of weakening or fatigue, as she stood in the unrelenting noonday heat.

"Retake." The makeup expert came forward to rearrange a strand of hair. A few seconds later the chief photographer left his camera. Taking Jill's chin in his hand, he swiveled her head as though she were made of plastic. A small, dapper man with a neat black mustache, he had to reach up to his model's face. Her smile never faltered.

"That's it—that's perfect. Hold it!" He returned to his camera.

You issued no commands; you had nothing to say, but the action revolved around you and everyone deferred to you, the impresario. Even Jill Boyd, the fabled leading lady of this traveling troupe, was a doll of your making. She was your brainchild; the entire advertising stunt was your invention, it would endure year after year. On Madison Avenue, you were proclaimed a genius; other brewers envied your "inspiration" and the public waited eagerly

each season for the election of the new Miss Meistersinger. The winner was on exhibition everywhere: on posters, lighting up dark saloons, in the
daily newspapers, she accompanied the traveler in
full, glossy color, on buses and subways—an all-
American girl, elected by popular ballot. A fresh
face appeared each year: blond, brunette, redhead,
all radiating the same wholesome glow and cas-
ualness; each one the descendant of the first Miss
Meistersinger, Jill Boyd. Their image was to become
as familiar as the features of the President himself.

Year after year, following the election, you and
your entourage traveled to an expensive resort location: Florida, Arizona, Bermuda, California, for
the "shooting." You returned, your heavy–jowled
face red as a cockscomb from the sun, your mind
filled with slogans and new ideas, on a vaster and
vaster scale. And the multiheaded, multibodied
American idol proliferated: on the tennis court, in
swing and hammock, the ski slope, sailboat and
divingboard—her lips forever parted in the famous
Meistersinger smile that glorified the superiority of
the product with the copyrighted printed boast: "My
beer is the smooth beer—Meistersinger."

Yet you never lost your heart to any of the candidates. Although you addressed all of them im-
partially with your old-fashioned gallantry, the
uncultivated daisy was not for you. You preferred
the orchidaceous hothouse bloom—the moon pal-
lor of Margo Duke, your wife.

In the summer I would occasionally visit High
Hill, your Westchester home. I went to see Margo,

knowing you would not be there, as business occupied you more and more and you moved from New York City to Brooklyn, to Los Angeles, where with an infusion of de la Riviere funds, you had, at last, realized your ambition to purchase a West Coast branch.

I usually found Margo alone. Aloof and ungregarious, with Duke away at a prestigious New England preparatory boarding school, she endured solitary, idle hours, consoled by the thought that it was all for the benefit of the only human being she loved without reservation. I was aware of the dissensions in your marriage, but my sympathies were with Margo and I chose to be her friend. At that time, furthermore, I was drawn by her beauty; the "angel of the house," abandoned, and the feminist not yet fully born—pulchritude in itself constituted a type of feminine virtue. And just as a young bit player looks up to a leading lady, I regarded Margo's physical perfection with admiration, wistful but without animus.

After five years of marriage, your home still seemed uninhabited. The spacious, sunken drawing room resembled an interior display of a department store. The sofas and easy chairs, upholstered in moss-green chintz with plump, pink cabbage roses, were smooth and shiny new. And the roses outside the French windows at the end of the long room appeared artificial, too. No one entered the little garden, its paths were frequented by birds: robins, sparrows, cardinals and goldfinches. At the center, surrounded by the neat flowerbeds, a cherub poured water from a jug into a circular basin. The splashing sound was nostalgic, reminiscent of a past that had been forgotten—or perhaps it was merely the background music of summer itself, the garden only a mirage outside the window. It waited to come alive; for Margo, its mistress, to tend it; but she rarely left the house.

She was usually found in the dark wood-paneled den. Over the mantel hung that photograph of Duke, enlarged so that the grin was still broader and the freckles magnified, more than lifesize. He had long outgrown that small-boy image, but Margo was comforted by the picture, and also the twilight in the den was kind to the faint marks of aging beginning to be visible in the candor of the outdoors.

One day, I found her not alone. I was introduced to two friends, ex-colleagues from her years as a model. Despite my entrance, they continued to slouch in positions of dejection, while Margo, like a schoolmistress dealing with problem pupils, sat straight-backed before them. Her intimacy with her former friends had cooled during her marriage; she had so little in common now with women who worked for a living. But she was sometimes consulted because of her cool intelligence, and was even urged to start an agency of her own. With her business sense and experience, backed by her husband's money, she should be able to make a success of it. But Margo clamped her firm jaw in opposition. Her single desire was to maintain a home for her son and, in her judgment, that did not include a career-minded mother. No—it was her choice to wait from school holiday to school holiday, grateful for the crumbs of time Duke could allot her from his busy social schedule. She provided this life for him, and she would pay the price with inflexible resignation. You, Nicholas, were elated by your stepson's conquests and you bragged about the country clubs where he was received, whose doors were firmly closed to you, a Jew. But it was never your way to capitulate and you regarded one of these bastions, a large 1920's monument to money, located just beyond the entrance to High Hill, as another territory to be conquered. In the meantime, you beamed at Duke, who turned away in sullen silence.

Margo always listened with sympathy to the troubles of her friends and was ready with advice.

"I'm all washed up as a model," Serena moaned. "He won't even give me a job as a receptionist or fashion consultant."

Serena had grown fat, her face was puffy from drink. But just as a ruin still suggests the palace originally there, through the flabby flesh the remains of her beauty were still visible.

Margo was quick to console and advise. Women in trouble were always able to arouse the mother instinct in her. "Why don't you try a health farm," she suggested, "you must fight back. If you need money, I will be glad to help. You still have the best profile of any of us."

"It's too late—and you know it," Serena wailed, dabbing at her reddened eyes with a damp handkerchief. Then, seeming to notice me for the first time, she apologized, "I'm sorry, I just don't seem able to get a hold of myself." And like a hopeless pupil, erasing and redoing the smudged sums on a blackboard, she dabbed and poked at her ravaged face in order to find the result she would never attain, the answer to her muddle: her former beauty.

Barbara, the second visitor, though past her prime, was still lovely, with a tumble of auburn curls and turquoise eyes. I gathered that she had been deserted by her husband. A situation of this kind never failed to bring out the female warrior in Margo. She briskly discussed lawyers, alimony, the ammunition of battle.

But Barbara was not listening. "I still love him. I could kill him," she said.

"Romantic nonsense," Margo snapped. "Pull yourself together, have some self-respect. No man is worth it—"

Barbara remained unresponsive. But Margo had determination for two. The male sex was the common enemy and, in unity, women could prevail.

The conversation was making me uncomfortable; I felt an intruder and although I disagreed with Margo, I remained silent. Compared to these women, I seemed youthfully inexperienced.

I got up to go. "I think I must leave," I said.

"Stay a little longer," Margo answered, "I was just going to get us some lemonade."

I sat down again, but my capitulation seemed craven; a disloyalty to my own feelings—and to my husband as well.

As though divining my thoughts, Margo turned

the brightness of her black eyes on me and remarked sagely, sadly, "I hope you never wake up, dear child."

She served the lemonade, her long white fingers with their pointed blood-red enameled, claw-like nails curled around the frosty pitcher. The strategy for war continued in the snug den.

Nicholas, you were the only male always exempted from Margo's band of brigands, perhaps because of your chronic sexual humility. But you were the enemy, too; your abject ways could be as degrading as the bestiality of the others. Sometimes you treated your wife as a gem smothered inside a velvet case; at other moments "Little Miss Margo" was petted and stroked like Duke's spaniel or the cat, overfed and now verging on middle age.

At last I was able to break away, and I hurried home. That night I dreamed I was back at High Hill in the same company. But we sat in the locked-out flower garden on painfully uncomfortable wrought-iron chairs. I was surprised to find myself admitted to this place, unpenetrated until then, a scenic backdrop beyond the drawing room window. I noticed that although it was midsummer, the edges of the rose petals were crisp and blackened as though prematurely nipped by frost. And, instead of the urn, the stone cherub was shouldering an icy pitcher of lemonade that trickled into the basin with a tantalizing, homesick sound.

From the silent house I heard a hollow clanking of iron braces and your voice calling, "Little Miss Margo, where are you?"

You appeared framed in the open French door of the drawing room. But dreams possess the honesty to discard the delusion of the orderly succession of time; and you were not your present gigantic self, preoccupied with matters of business, but the skinny, shunned adolescent with the wild, terrified eyes of a runaway horse.

"Little Miss Margo, answer me," you pleaded.

A house finch, finely wrought as a Fabergé jeweled bird, alighted on the chilly pitcher. Its claws, blood-red, hooked to the rim—it regarded me with bright defiant black eyes. At that moment I realized that Margo was absent, she had never been with the rest of us in the pretty, lonely little flower garden.

I woke with a start, my dream still intact; as real as my husband sleeping by my side, his stentorian breathing calm and rhythmic. Out of doors, the myriad insects of summer were chanting in chorus,

"I hope you never wake up—I hope you never wake up—dear child," they warned me over and over again.

The dark of December twilight in the city streets to this very day holds a promise—a sense of joyous expectation—with which no pastoral spring can compare. From a long distance I see three figures, distinct and portentous; the repetitive symbols of ritual—you and I, Nicholas, with the tall form of my French governess between us. She was bundled in so many layers of clothing that the body beneath was smothered out of existence. Mademoiselle's spinsterhood was so impenetrable that one could

not picture her naked; her correct French-Swiss vocabulary lacked all words to express the biological
functions, they were banned by her *politesse*, as her
physical person was obscured by its somber swad-
dlings. Sometimes I wondered whether Mademoiselle, handsome and stately (as much as one could
see of her), might be hiding some deformity, an
abnormality too hideous to name.

But on Christmas Eve when Mother sent us out
to wander the neighborhood streets while she com-
pleted, in secret, the final preparations, even the
lumpy figure of Mademoiselle was invested with
ceremony, each lamppost raised its electric globe
like a halo and the windows of the stores along
Madison Avenue, still open for last–minute cus-
tomers, were miniature stages as fascinating as the
tableaus of the Nativity Pageant at school. We were
on our way to call on Madame Julia Nicolier, the
dry cleaner, a friend of Mademoiselle's. This, too,
was an invariable part of the evening's procedure.
On ordinary days, Madame Nicolier and her estab-
lishment appeared commonplace, but on Christmas
Eve, the steam from her iron filled the room with
diaphanous clouds, through which her rosy face
peered, meaningful as that of the Annunciation
Angel's.

We marched in step along our route, which was
sometimes powdered by a light snowfall. The sky
hung low, pregnant with treasure never revealed
to human eye. When the heavens were rent, the
secret hoard would scatter over the earth and bless
us all. While I waited, I sometimes even joined

hands with you, my brother, as the three of us trotted up Madison Avenue toward Seventy-second Street.

Now I realize that, in all probability, you never shared my ignorant jubilation. Although we both looked forward to all the presents we would receive beneath the tree, I remember that you would loiter at the portals of a church along the way. Although the door was always open, we never entered; but you stopped to look inside at the flickering candles. Were you already longing for admittance? Were you experiencing a feeling of exclusion I did not yet realize existed?

In our library, chapel to the living room, the main sanctuary where the Christmas tree reigned in glory, Mother, at her piano, led us in song; all the familiar favorites that brought a lump into my throat: "Silent Night," "Adeste Fidelis," "Away in a Manger," "The First Noel." From the living room emanated a faint yet intoxicating whiff of dry pine needles, and I wished this moment would last forever. I did not know that our celebration was an empty charade. And just as Mademoiselle by her odd assortment of wrappings denied the presence of the flesh-and-blood woman beneath them, my family's deliberate avoidance of our own culture and religion, even as we observed the birth of Christ in carols— joyous, solemn and mysterious—attempted to bury an unwanted truth, the fact of our Jewish heritage. But I believe, for you, Nicholas, even at an early age, this homemade reverence did not suffice. Excessive in all things, you always ventured further than the rest of your circle and your family. Through the open door of a church on our twilight walks on the eve of Christmas, you beheld, worshipfully, the flicker of votive candles and smelled the antique, sweet aroma of real incense. Jewish self-hatred would eventually propel you across the threshold to a place within. Years later, in lone repudiation of your kind, you became a Catholic.

This occurred at a period during which I saw you rarely. Margo never mentioned it and I can only imagine my father's revulsion and fury at your act. Although for two generations before him, my father's paternal elders had done their best to shed every vestige of Jewishness, the accompanying atheism was as zealous as the dogma of a religious bigot. When I was a small child my grandfather, aged ninety, a rosy, white-bearded Santa Claus, boasted about this traditional atheism in the same spirit he showed when exhibiting his upper arm muscles, acquired at seventeen when he was apprenticed to a cooper.

My father would exclaim as he regarded me with pride and pleasure, "We can do without all those fairy stories. Religion is for the weak—the stupid!"

One lived and died as good burghers enjoying, to the fullest, the fruits of this earth; scoffing at the fancies that had invented the "soul" and "immortality." With the Bloch genes one could expect to endure to a ripe old age, but when the time was up, one took one's leave, with regret, but facing with stolid fortitude the unadorned advent of total extinction.

For his son to break with this heritage by becoming a Catholic, was, in my father's eyes, a transgression as terrible as when in a pious family a member turns apostate. I can hear him shouting, as he so often did when provoked by you, repeating that word, the only one that came to mind in his rage, "Don't be an *idiot!*"

How was it possible that he had produced this wayward, hysterical giant? But you could never be deterred; whether it was a matter of buying a West Coast brewery, an exorbitantly expensive automobile, a bride—or embracing the Papist faith—your will prevailed. You left your small, dynamic parent in your wake, wrathful on the exterior, while deep down, the blind Old Testament love of father for son remained undisturbed.

It is my belief that you were drawn to Catholicism, the matrix Christian faith, because of its elaborate mysticism, and also because, in a Protestant nation, it kept you in the minority. But your insecurity never blocked your march toward total assimilation.

I have often paused before the Gothic facade, unremarkable in every way, of the church where you received instruction. As children we had seen, on our summer European trips, the architectural marvels of historic cathedrals, yet we had never been inside a synagogue any place on earth. We were excluded from what was rightfully ours as well as from that which belonged to others. Now, just as a despised illegitimate child may be received at last, as a member of a great family, you had found a home. I see you walking down the gloomy halls of the parish house that, like our first school, smelled of varnish and disinfectant. But there is hope in your heart. Timidly, you knock on your instructor's door; the pearly gate through which you would enter the church, shedding on the threshold the ugly, detested raiment of your Jewishness.

In my mind's eye I picture Father Duffy in his long dusty black skirt and clerical collar. He is not an imposing figure like the Reverend Knowlton at Wellington Academy. Father Duffy does not resemble a Gothic saint but, rather, the policeman on the block. He is young, hardly older than you, with dead white skin, glossy black hair and small intense blue eyes under heavy dark brows that look as artificial as a false mustache. His lips are thick, sensual, his chin, weak; one can imagine that, for him, the mortification of the flesh is a weighty task to be resumed each day. Yet the blue, deep-set eyes are keen and you are an apt pupil. With your ability to memorize anything—a telephone directory, a train schedule—religious instruction presented no difficulties and it was not long before you left that unassuming edifice on the Upper East Side, no longer a Jew, but a newly baptized Christian convert.

At home, Margo took no notice of the event and every Sunday you attended the local, suburban Catholic church by yourself. There was no more lolling around the house in your bathrobe and scuffed bedroom slippers, your long heron-like legs exposed and bare. Neatly dressed in your Wellington blue blazer, you went to Mass. Although you knew none of your coreligionists, you had advanced since your boarding school days, when you sat in chapel and only dreamed of belonging. Now, despite your aloneness, in the eyes of the Catholic hierarchy, in the view of God himself, you had been accepted. And, as you lowered your tall, cumbersome body to kneel on the hard floor of the pew, I am certain that no other member of the flock prayed with more fervor, sincerity and credulousness than you.

The route of memory is not uniformly open. Along the way one comes across discoveries as well as dead ends, areas erased by time: like the picture books I used to find in my Christmas stocking in which the image was made to disappear by the pressure of a magic crayon. The 1950's between the war years, and the rebellious sixties, have all but vanished. When I attempt to bring them back, for some mysterious reason and despite our distant connection, I see, most clearly, Sebastian Duke, Margo's son. He has, by now, graduated from school and is about to enter Princeton in the fall. You have just given him a silvery Chrysler convertible and I picture him at the wheel of his car—a handsome princeling, as his name suggests. He is slender and he retained his mother's perfection of feature, but his ears jut slightly, a virile flaw—like Clark Gable's. Duke was "popular" with both boys and girls, but he appeared always cool and elusive with that faintly disdainful look in his granite eyes. You talked endlessly about his athletic successes and his amatory conquests. They seemed to compensate for your own adolescent failures. Proudly, you would show visitors to High Hill the trophy room filled with Duke's silver cups, medals and blue ribbons. You seemed to take more pleasure in them than did their owner, who merely shrugged and remained silent. But your volubility covered everything, while Margo and Duke shared their quiet intimacy; it was an indication of their blood-tie as opposed to your foreignness. You drew vicarious pleasure from the debutante parties and country club dances attended by your stepson. It was Duke who penetrated that impregnable club next door that had been closed to you for so many years. But still, you did not give up, you continued to try—there was always another influential contact, some new "pull." You admired Duke's girlfriends and earnestly evaluated their beauty as though they were Miss Meistersinger contestants. Yet it had not been suburban belles you had aspired to as you watched, from the sidelines, at Wellington Academy "proms." You dreamed more ambitiously.

When I observed your adopted son, his nonchalance and easy grace, I thought of your very different adolescence in another society. Perhaps that is why his handsome face remains in memory as I search for the vanished 1950's. But when I hear, today, a Cole Porter song, an earlier time breaks through into the present. The crooning contains old loves and hopes in its lilting measures and I am transported to a section of the route not yet engulfed in forgetfulness.

The white orchid on the strap of my mother's evening gown quivered like a butterfly about to take wing. She was standing with the rest of my family in the receiving line of my "coming out" party at the Plaza Hotel. The preparations for this Yuletide season of social activity had been frenetic and even my mother had taken pains with her costume for this night. That afternoon, Miss Nelly, tall and thin as a scarecrow, dressed in black and carrying a black doctor's satchel with her implements, arrived at our home. With her curling irons she corrugated my mother's long, straight gray-blond hair and pinned it in an unfashionable bun at the nape of her neck.

In the receiving line, I was too excited and absorbed with myself and the impression I was making on others to notice my mother's incandescent beauty. In my white tulle dress with silver kid trim, like the orchid on my mother's shoulder, I was on the verge of flight. In preparation for this season, there had been orgies of shopping: to this day, I recall each gown with its individual personality, every one a lost friend, not forgotten. There was the scarlet velveteen, a Christmas angel, the black taffeta with coquettish magenta flounces, a flamenco dancer, and the white tulle for this occasion, a preview of the bride I would be before long. Just as the hunter returns, victorious with his prey, the young women of the circle and their parents would be rewarded for their efforts by capturing a husband. Cloaked in gauzy white, plushy red or sleek black, I was lost in my finery: I was what I wore.

That winter, the balls proliferated. One after the other, the Jewish debutantes were introduced. Later there was dancing all through the night. The males,

in "full dress," swooped onto the floor like pred-
atory birds; unaware that it was they, in fact, who
constituted the catch. Dancing, the girls prayed
that they would be "cut in" on often, that they
would be "popular"—which meant that there could
be no more than one circle around the slippery
floor before your partner was dismissed by that
white-gloved tap upon his shoulder and you were
transferred to other arms. The pristine gowns were
soon crushed, their hems torn by heavy, sometimes maladroit male feet. But the largest and
clumsiest were yours, Nicholas. In the "stag line"
you were conspicuous; though stooped, the tallest,
a Mount Everest among lesser peaks, all topped
by snowy stiff collars and white bow ties. When
you danced with me, one tentacle arm crushed my
back, the other pumped arrhythmically up and
down. Like a deaf man you were oblivious to the
seductive strains of the famous band. You even
closed your eyes to the gyrating couples (causing
collisions), the better to concentrate on the chatter
you delivered into my ear.

"Did you notice all the foreign cars parked outside the hotel?" "I wonder what this affair costs?"
"—but with that 'man in the White House'—" "the
'Commies'—the 'Commies'—they're everywhere,
maybe even here—"

I worried that the carefully prepared showcase
of my person would be ruffled by my aversion to
you and your disruptive soliloquy. Surely my intense relief, after the deliverance of that tap on your
shoulder and your return to the periphery, was
obvious. Fortunately, you rarely ventured out onto

the dance floor, preferring to remain apart, dreaming of better things.

For you did not forget that the bedecked, sweet-smelling debutantes, their hardworking parents, the formal, eligible young men were tainted. Jews, all of us, we were confined in a gilded ghetto behind a high wall of prejudice. At this moment, along Fifth Avenue, the real debutantes, the Gentile ones, were receiving their Gentile guests in similar ballrooms. Through chinks in the wall, we had observed them, and like amnesiacs, we were no longer certain who we were, where we came from, what we knew. With the advantage of wealth and the meticulous cultivation of the traditions, customs, culture, the outward aspect of the others, perhaps, in time, the wall might crumble. We would be released into a joyful mingling, everyone on equal terms, Jew and Gentile become as one. Until then, we made do with our separate but parallel society. There were, of course, the exceptions, the ultra-privileged, who had already managed to squeeze through the small openings, to make a tentative start on the other side.

You, unlike your family, were not resigned to waiting. Future generations did not concern you personally; you were determined to get there yourself. With your scared green-brown eyes, always closed to what you did not want to see, your body, precariously balanced, you, who as a child, used to quake before the miniature ladder of a slide, were determined to scale the wall and put an end to your alienation.

But alienation and loneliness, like the wicked

witches, were to dog your footsteps. Though increasingly prodded by the ugly pair, with your optimism and stubbornness, you continued to believe that the next pace would gain for you the liberation you desired.

I do not know the facts surrounding Margo's defection, but I imagine that after eight years of marriage to you—with Duke embarked in the proper direction—she was no longer able to keep her end of the bargain. She had come to the limit of her endurance; she left you.

You told me about it on the telephone; looking back I marvel at your steadfast loyalty to me, your confidence in my affection, while I was pulling away from you with all my might. It would make me squirm inwardly when a mutual acquaintance said, "I have just seen your brother and he told me that you and he have always had a wonderful relationship—so rare these days when families tend to fall apart . . ."

"Margo has left me," you told me with a note of hysteria in your voice, but no rancor. There was sorrow and shock, but perhaps, knowing you, a touch of hope also. The right bait in the trap might induce Margo to come back.

But she never returned. With your usual lavish generosity, you provided her with an expensive eyrie in a fashionable neighborhood, overlooking a view of the jagged skyline of lower Manhattan. You continued to live alone at High Hill. Fortunately, you were occupied with brewery matters, in Brooklyn and Los Angeles, and the Bloch liaison with their partners, the de la Rivieres, flourished. Furthermore, the de la Riviere clan was as reactionary politically as you and shared your allegiance to General Franco. As the genial progenitor of Miss Meistersinger, who was still beloved by the public, you went on "location" twice a year and continued to be consulted and respected as a creative thinker in advertising. But at night you returned to the empty house. You felt affection for its rosy brick, ivy-covered facade, the chintzes, the snug den, spiral staircase and, your favorite, the pearly oval dining room—they were the possessions of which Margo once had been your most highly prized.

I know that Father objected to your unnecessary generosity to a disloyal wife. But, just as during your green youth, the clash between you was caused not by the gulf of a generation so much as by your wild romanticism opposed to his pragmatic worldliness. Was Father reminded of his cousin Daniel and his courtly, unrealistic, profligate homage to worthless women? Did I think of him at that time, or is it only now that I merge the small, gnarled, ancient figure of Daniel with your gigantic cumbersome form? In my mind's eye I see this composite wooer on bended knee, offering some unloving woman an old-fashioned bouquet—his innocent heart.

In my efforts to disentangle myself from you, loyal to Margo, I paid her a visit soon after the separation. In her high, antiseptic apartment she appeared cool, unruffled and I still marveled at the perfection of her face. On closer inspection, however, the papery dryness of her white skin was apparent despite her carefully applied makeup. Her shapely painted mouth was harder, the lips less full. Their deep red shape filled my vision, suddenly separate from the rest of her person, and I felt a flicker of penetrating awareness as though another existence was attempting to break through the opaque veil of present time in an instant of déjà vu. It passed, but later I recalled that dream; the roses in the garden at High Hill, pinched and tipped by frost in the middle of summer.

I asked Margo about her plans.

"I have none," she answered.

Would she just waste herself here, too? Removed from High Hill, would she remain a prisoner in her new shiny modern cage? It was obvious she was still living for those telephone calls and for the few hours Duke might spare on weekends between trips to and from girls' colleges.

"I have promised myself," she went on as though reading my mind, "that next year, when Duke is a senior, I will start going out again with men. Until then . . ." her voice trailed off.

Neither of us gave any thought to a career, despite her ability and the unusual fact that "going out with men" sounded like a burden prompted by conventionality rather than inclination—a duty postponed until a vague "tomorrow."

We kissed good-bye lightly at the threshold of her box-like, fireproof doorway, as friendly as we had been in the neo-Georgian entrance to High Hill. It was only after the visit, Nicholas, that I realized your name had not been uttered by either of us.

The accident occurred during Duke's senior year, at night, on a road between Princeton and Vassar. It was your gift, the silvery convertible, that killed him. The funeral was attended by handsome boys and girls, his friends. The coffin, smothered in white roses, was carried by a select group of youths with stunned, pale faces. My fading picture of Duke, his casual grace and inscrutable gray eyes, blurred into elegiac poetry . . . *I weep for Adonais, he is dead.* . . .

But Margo, dry-eyed, blade-thin, steely stiff, the husk of herself, and you, Nicholas, sobbing as you lumbered down the aisle to a front pew, were real—shocking as the sight of the fatal accident itself.

THREE

THE INTRODUCTION OF YOUR NEW BRIDE CAUSED A ripple of astonishment to pass through the sameness of Sunday lunch at Father's. The dining room was unaltered since my childhood: the window, still curtained to shut out the view of the ugly brick wall of the adjacent apartment building, made a perpetual night even at midday; the silver tea service, highly polished though unused now, standing like deposed royalty upon the sideboard; and, over the Oriental screen in front of the swinging pantry door, miniature Chinese figures continued to scramble up the impregnable sides of a conical golden mountain. The guests, for the most part, were invariable also, and a quiver of shock passed among them at first sight of your conquest, the film actress Ramona Randall.

The story of the courtship was recounted to me by an old friend who had been witness to it. With retelling, it has become legend, fantastic as a tale from the *Arabian Nights*. My venerable informer, a painter, had been visiting at a ranch house on the outskirts of Santa Fe owned by a fellow artist and his wife, a sculptor. The low adobe home crouched in the deep dun-colored wrinkles of the bare land, its primeval severity unrelieved by either tree or flower. Inside, the host, hostess and their friends, who included Ramona Randall, reclined on cushions (handwoven by natives) scattered over the terra cotta floor. It was said that the actress had some Indian and Spanish blood in her veins, so she might have been more indigenous to the scene than her refugee companions for whom this place represented a deliberate stand against the "artificiality" of city life. The conversation was lively and, just as at a revivalist meeting the faithful rally around the incorporeal presence of God and praise Him, here in the adobe ranch house, Art in all its manifestations was volubly worshipped, Ramona Randall representing a masterpiece in the flesh among the more abstract examples in clay, metal and paint.

Suddenly the tapping of pellets falling on the roof made itself audible above the excited buzz of talking.

"Hail," someone announced.

But the sky had remained flawless blue, the sun blazed. Perhaps this abnormal occurrence was a sign from nature announcing an apocalypse which only this group of artists would survive. But a small plane was visible, circling the house. Colored stones were dropping from it, flashing emerald-green, ruby-red, sapphire-blue, a profusion of gems ignited by the sun. They bombarded the roof and fell to the drab ground. At last the flimsy one-engine craft landed on a flat strip near the ranch. A figure rose with difficulty in the cramped cabin. His height and bulk made him seem to be disassembling the parts of his body, and just like the Meccano-Set toy in a box beneath the Christmas tree, the sections were put together to form a whole as he emerged. There you stood, Nicholas. Your habitual fears overcome in your picaresque pursuit, you were the creator of the artificial accident of nature, the stubborn wooer of the reluctant princess inside the adobe castle.

The reeducation of Father took another leap, but not without the usual preliminary protests, growls, exclamations and hurling of epithets. Despite the miraculous rain of fake jewels, Ramona Randall still demurred. Now you took it into your head that your advances were compromising her, she should not be seen with a man not yet divorced. Immediate proceedings were imperative; your lawyers were recalled and Margo's, victors by default, were able to negotiate a settlement so unfair that, in good times and bad, it would leave you financially crippled for the rest of your days. Father was forced to come to the rescue with supplementary funds. He regarded the naïveté and improvidence of his son with incredulous despair. The squandering of money on women, from Candida Blanche to Margo Duke to Ramona Randall, was growing to such proportions that, for the first time, he feared for the future. Again, was Father reminded of cousin Daniel?— Daniel calling daily on his wife in the costly sanatorium, convinced, to the end, of her perfection and her worthiness of love; Daniel, the twisted knight with his courtly offerings of sweets wrapped in jewel-colored tinfoil, his fedora at a rakish angle, plume-less, but always ready to be doffed in the presence of the weaker sex—the lonely knight dwelling with his fantasies in the vastness of his room at the Pick-wick Arms. But it was doubtful that Father thought of Daniel at all.

"Ramona needs me," you wailed, and brought out tricks for getting your way, variations of the method you had employed since childhood. At the rumbling outset of an argument, I could almost see again your fingers down your convulsed throat, the rise of mercury in a thermometer placed against a hot light bulb. . . . The divorce was speedily granted, Ramona Randall's objections for unknown reasons, overcome, and you were married in the Catholic faith this time. The civil ceremony with Margo had been rendered null.

The "faithful" at Sunday lunch included "Aunt" Maud, my mother's lifelong friend, and her spin-ster daughter. Maud was an aging Edwardian-type beauty with violet eyes (as in romantic novels), and a dyed reddish, frizzled bang. She had been di-vorced years before from a scion of the prominent Thalheim family, and though she reviled her ex-husband, she continued to cherish his name; it often acted as a pass to resort hotels which customarily excluded Jews. Dolph Dubois, a Frenchman, had been a Columbia classmate of Father's; now ren-dered mute by a stroke, he was obliged to com-municate via pad and pencil. But he was always jovial—a small, rounded person, with cheeks veined the color of *vin rosé*, he manipulated his writing

equipment cheerfully, with the dexterity of a vet-
eran waiter taking down an order. Dr. Fritz Buhler
was German, half Jewish, distinguished by a deep
slash bisecting his lower lip, a dueling scar from his
former life as a student at Heidelberg. This old
wound, like a decoration in his buttonhole, emphasized the doctor's Teutonic fairness and mini-
mized the Semitic arch of his large nose, lending
his appearance, in our eyes, an ambassadorial dignity. Sometimes Dr. Helmuth Schneider, the American representative of the de la Rivieres, his wife
Amalia and daughter Ursula came to lunch. Exile
had not altered Dr. Schneider, nor moderated his
German accent. But his attitude to you, Nicholas,
had grown noticeably less obsequious and somewhat resembled that of the disciplinarian father that
you never had.

It was nearly two o'clock and Ramona Randall
had not yet made her entrance. She was a late sleeper,
you explained, and also there were all those calls
concerning roles in films. The trans-Atlantic wires
hummed, you bragged—Paris, Rome, Madrid,
London, Athens, Berlin, Istanbul . . . The Sunday
roast beef would be overcooked; Father ordered his
guests to sit down to table. You began to expound
one of your favorite incendiary topics: the recent
Senator McCarthy hearings. You held forth noisily,
words rushing from your mouth. You would close
your eyes as you talked, as though in your vehemence your senses were confounded, and not to see
meant not to hear any objections or interruptions
to your discourse. Dr. Schneider, although a polit-

ical right-winger himself, watched you, his heavy melancholy blue eyes registering mute disapproval.

". . . 'witch hunting.' It's much too mild. . . . The Reds should be deported, every one, to the Soviet Union where they belong. This country must rid itself of Stalinist sympathizers—only yesterday, I was speaking to the Spanish Ambassador, and he told me . . ."

I had heard it all before—the fanaticism, the name dropping, but it could still arouse my anger as well as a sense of personal shame that resembled one of those nightmares in which one is revealed as an accomplice to a shameful act or discovered in a condition of indecent exposure.

At this point, you were silenced and you opened your eyes as your wife entered the room. The guests gasped inwardly. Ramona Randall was still dressed in bedroom negligée, her long dark hair was wavy and tumbled. In the snowy white valley between her neck and shoulder, there nestled a wizened, miniature marmoset. She was holding a tall glass of colorless liquid that I took to be water—learning only later that it was gin. Unlike Margo Duke, Ramona Randall had a full, voluptuous body. She reminded me of one of Raphael's blooming peasant models before she had been transformed through his art into a vision of the Virgin Mary. Everything about her was physically generous: she was tall and had full breasts, a large perfectly proportioned oval face and brown eyes, both wide and long, like a detail magnified out of the general composition of a canvas. Her healthful aspect was deceptive, however. You would always be drawn to "damsels in distress"; it was your pleasure to console them for their past sorrows, and Ramona Randall was another wounded soul. But the nature of her injury always remained a mystery. It was rumored that she had an inoperable obstruction that made normal sexual intercourse impossible, that she was a lesbian or warped by some primitive, guilty inhibition acquired during her early Catholic upbringing.

My encounters with Ramona Randall were few; she traveled a great deal and her stopovers between trips were short. Therefore our meeting on a certain New Year's Eve remains a puzzle. It stands out in memory with clarity and illogicality, lacking preamble or epilogue. And, just as in a painting by Salvador Dali in which a misshapen watch, a conch shell, one breast with a jeweled nipple and a skull may be strewn in haphazard juxtaposition along a stretch of beach, the components of those bizarre hours, apparently senseless, retain a hidden significance for me.

Our house was situated only a few minutes away from High Hill. In winter it was, alternately, hot and cold. The wind sobbed and blustered through its many windows. While the old-fashioned hearths blazed bravely, the heating system, like a forgetful janitor, willing but incurably absentminded, worked overtime in some rooms, while others remained chilled and forgotten, the cheerful chintzes of summer drooped forlornly in the conservatory steaminess.

You were late as usual and when the front door opened, or rather was blown out by the gale, you were ready with your usual glib alibis.

"A thousand apologies," you began, and there followed the long list: business obligations at the last moment, a tangle of unfortunate delays, none of them your fault. Your gaiety as well as your excuses rang false. This was to be merely a pre-midnight drink together before we both went off to other places. Why, poor clown, could you never be casual, less conspicuous, loud-mouthed, groveling? I comforted myself with the reminder that in the world of commerce you were admired as the originator of Miss Meistersinger, who continued to beam upon the populace, and who owed her existence to you.

Ramona was already showing signs of inebriation. She was wearing a Mexican peasant dress, the gauzy blouse inflating the ripe fullness of her breasts, the wide bodice tightly laced above many layers of flounced multicolored skirts—a goddess bag lady! When I commented on her costume, she exclaimed, "You must have one like it! Lots of them. When I go to Mexico, I will buy them for you. What size do you wear? No, better try mine on—"

She insisted that I undress and she did the same in the chilly bedroom. Ramona drank frequently from the tall glass that, by this time, I knew to be gin. As she helped me into the filmy blouse, the numerous, swinging native skirts, her hands were caressing. Although she tipsily sang my praises, in her dress I could not help feeling like a grocery store pear bedecked in the ill-fitting skin of an exotic, tropical pomegranate.

Hypocrites, we drank champagne in comradeship; only you, who had learned young to ignore the nuances of other people's feelings, were sincere in your genial, impersonalized good will. But you looked strangely effaced and pale. By this time your wife, thoroughly drunk, was breaking glasses and throwing kisses to an invisible audience.

"Darling," you ventured, "I think we should go. Chee Chee must be lonely without you." Perhaps the thought of her pet marmoset might touch her.

Ramona rose unsteadily to her feet. She made no move to leave, but looked down at you. Arms akimbo, fury flashing from her eyes like New Year's Eve sparklers, Carmen in flame, she screamed, "Shut up! I don't give a fuck about Chee Chee, you or your whole fucking family!" There was a pause, and with a raucous laugh, she added, "Look at him! And he calls himself a man!"

Despite the fact that I had entertained similar thoughts about you, her insult cut deep into my entrails.

You finally managed to propel Ramona, still shouting, toward the front door. Before disappearing into the blustery darkness outside, you turned back and called, jauntily, "Happy New Year, everyone!", setting a jolly party cap upon the disheveled and derelict evening.

I learned later that when you returned home, Ramona attacked you physically, attempting to stab you with a carving knife. I visualized her chasing you around the kitchen table, brandishing the weapon. I recognized from childhood that look of terror in your brown-green eyes, as you fell down before her, sobbing, imploring. You were the supplicant again, confronted over and over by your tormentor in different guises.

The following day, New Year's, Ramona remained in bed and you nursed her with freshly squeezed soothing, sweet orange juice. . . . In the stable at Green Meadows the horse's large brown, uncomprehending eyes were wild and treacherous, but the gardener said, "Don't be afraid, Master Nicholas." And you held out your hand to the beast who had thrown you and stomped upon you, offering your lump of sugar in a gesture of timid reconciliation. . . .

Another family reunion, I believe the last in which Ramona Randall took part, was set again at our country home. It was July, and the rooms were irradiated all day by the reliable position of the sun. Now you, Father, Ramona, my husband, and I sat on the terrace watching the blood-red orb as it sank into the western sky. How often had I observed this wide panorama, a celestial kaleidescope in vermillion, fading pink with shifting cloud formations, shading from dark gray to white, tinged by fire and dying with the arrival of twilight? I was witness to the passing of one more day, a spectacle of which I never tired. Yet it held a core of melancholy within its splendor, demonstrating the steady inexorable passage of time. On our left, the moon appeared, modest and pale, and at the center of the dark backdrop, the evening star—magnified, phosphorescent green—pioneered the firmament in advance of its kind. The howling, sobbing wind seemed unbelievable now; instead, one heard a chorus of birds in motley song, sweet, sharp, atonal.

As in a play by Chekhov, we took our places on the garden terrace scene and the homey repetitiveness made up the drama. We spoke our lines into the vastness of the night and our voices were like the cicadas' incessant chatter during their brief life span in the dry grasses of summer.

"It's going to be hot tomorrow. The sun went down red."

"I think I'll go to the city on the train. I must—"

"I see a shooting star."

"Too early."

"A firefly—"

"Where?"

Chekhov's perennial visiting doctor was missing from our script, so Father played the role. He looked the part with his homely, humorous face, small, wise green eyes, and country squire clothes. As always, he seemed unrelated to you, his gigantic, sprawling son, whom he regarded with a blend of exasperation and pride. His attitude to Ramona Randall was mixed, also. In his seventies now, he was still a connoisseur of beautiful women, but in theory and practice he stubbornly held to the credo of his youth; he continued to winnow the wives from the mistresses, the actresses and others. Although he was carefully polite to Ramona, I felt the coolness and—just as someone cocooned in a snug room is sensitive to the slightest draft from outside—I resented Ramona for causing this almost imperceptible alteration in my father's customary warmth.

You, Nicholas, the irrepressible, noticed nothing. You were in high good humor this evening, as you and your wife were awaiting the hour to leave for the airport to receive the newborn infant being delivered to you for adoption. You kept glancing nervously at your Cartier watch. Ramona seemed pensive. Like the cruel wind of New Year's Eve, the smoldering virago had vanished as though she had never been. Ramona was now made up in pale, moonlit tones and her wild, dark, shoulder-length hair had been tamed, parted serenely in the center. The great brown eyes were ruminative. In floating blue drapery Raphael's painted Madonna had come to life.

"We have decided to name her Henrietta, after you," you were saying to Father, who made no response.

I knew that his loyalty was only to his own flesh and blood, to others he could be obtusely selfish. Adoption was an unnatural act and despite the disagreements and all the troubles you had caused, he wanted most of all a continuation of you, his own seed, his son.

"Her background is English, Irish and Dutch," you went on, "so she will probably be a blonde. I do hope she is pretty."

I knew you were already seeing the contrasting beauties of your wife and daughter—Rose Red and Snow White.

At last it was time to leave for the airport. In your

clumsy eagerness you stumbled. Ramona followed slowly. She was to have only a brief glimpse of her daughter as she was going to London the next day for the making of a costume film in which she would have the role of a Restoration barmaid who rises to become a favorite of the king.

I believe that her exit that night was her final one for me. I cannot recall seeing her again and I learned that, upon her return from London, deciding that, after all, a baby would not cement the crumbling marriage, she refused to sign the adoption papers. I could hear your pleas. "But she is ours!" And Ramona's retort, "Send her back, I have changed my mind."

But it was Ramona Randall who disappeared soon after this. Henrietta was not to be returned.

FOUR

YOU SHOWED AS LITTLE RANCOR FOLLOWING RAMONA'S defection as you had after Margo's. You spoke of both women as though they were wayward children, forgiven and, apparently, only remotely regretted. You had battled to keep one, then the other, but when they had finally gone you transferred your hysterical, demonstrative affections to the baby Henrietta. From your great height you would look down upon the small bundle, in ruffled lacy wrappings inside her bassinet and exclaim, "Isn't she beautiful!" adding, "I am sure she's going to be a blonde—her ancestry is one hundred percent Nordic."

Henrietta and her nanny lived with you at High Hill, without benefit of blood ties and, for a time, also without adoption papers. But she was your daughter instantly, and your love for her was to be a constant as long as you lived. At this period you were obliged to travel on business connected with Meistersinger's West Coast brewery, and during those absences the baby took up an abode at Father's apartment in New York City. You chose Mother's abandoned bedroom for the nursery because it was the largest. It was presided over by the nanny. These boarders made a change in Father's bachelor existence, but he took it with good humor. He would visit his infant namesake in the morning before going to his office and again when he returned at her bedtime. His manner was warm, yet it had a touch of formality when compared with memories of our childhood or the beaming pride he exhibited in the presence of my son. Had he overcome his objections to adoption or was he merely capitulating again to your eccentric ways? In any case, Henrietta's appearances continued at the apartment, where she arrived surrounded by the costliest infant's trousseau and piles of toys you provided. In the sunny nursery, twelve floors above the muffled roar of the subterranean trains and the noise of traffic, parented by two men, she reminded me of "The Luck of Roaring Camp" on Park Avenue.

Despite your painful childhood, you wished to recreate for your daughter the trappings of your early life. Were you, in essence, attempting to secure for Henrietta the goals of your unrealized dreams? And did you think that, just as a child on a carousel begs for one more ride in order to capture the golden ring that seems forever out of reach, Henrietta, seated upon her painted rocking horse, might one day grasp the prize never quite attained by yourself?

"That is the way it used to be," you insisted again and again.

In Mother's room, the chaste dressing table, the

couch on which I had found her, white and exhausted, shortly before her death, all the polished solid reproductions of eighteenth-century English furniture were crowded by the paraphernalia of pampered infancy. Your prodigious memory extended back to when you were six months old, recollections following one another in sequence like the records in Mother's handwriting in our Baby Books, still standing on a library shelf, the snapshot on each opening page a newborn stretched upon the starched knees of its nurse, mirrored now by the sight of Henrietta resting on the uniformed lap of her nanny.

Although the rear of the apartment was dusted every day, it remained unoccupied. Nothing in the old, deserted nursery had been moved or taken away. From its place on the wall, the black-and-white reproduction of Raphael's *Madonna of the Chair* still held sway. The Virgin continued to gaze placidly over the curly head of the infant Jesus, while a youthful John the Baptist looked on. The trio, within a circular design, were enclosed as in a holy womb. This picture was as familiar to our childhood as was the Lord's Prayer, which we mumbled senselessly before sleep. The inappropriateness of these Christian borrowings for Jewish children occurred to me later, but I am certain that our atheist father knew nothing of our nighttime ritual. It had probably been initiated by some pious nurse intent on saving our little heathen souls. Mother, however, did not object, her constant fears for her children made her superstitious and, who knew, the prayer might serve as an incantation to ward off dangers never far away. But I believe that her choice of the *Madonna of the Chair* was neither religious nor aesthetic, but emotional. The young female drew her; uncomfortable herself in the maternal role, more at home in her library and music room than the nursery, she may have hoped that her children would benefit from the unflagging calm regard of the Madonna cloaked in ideal nurturing.

And you, Nicholas, despite your adherence to "everything just as it used to be," did not remove the lithograph from the vacated room to Henrietta's quarters. As a practicing Catholic you spurned the half measures of the partially assimilated Jew.

At this period I saw you as rarely as possible. Our paths, our concerns had diverged, and no less than in childhood, you could still make me cringe, ashamed of myself through you. I trusted that not seeing you would be like not having a brother at all. But you, always impervious, would repeat far and wide, "My sister and I have all our lives been unusually close!"

Because we were so often apart, I must fill the gaps with inventions in writing this history, and these fictions have grown as real to me as the hours actually spent in your company; so profound are the alterations of memory, at once eroded and embroidered by the lengthening lapse of the years.

The hotel in Southern California was the most lavish in the area. Constructed during the 1920's, it boasted a splendid swimming pool in a neo-Spanish patio where potted palms, orange trees and oleanders bloomed, as in a Metro-Goldwyn-Mayer version of Eden. Like certain modish bars and restaurants in New York City this was a meeting place for big business; and as in those dining places where certain tables—at the rear or in the front—are strictly held for celebrities, the side of the pool with the cabañas was reserved for those with the greatest reputations. There, Nicholas, you could be found, the advertising "genius" inventor of the now mythological Miss Meistersinger, the forward-thinking baron of beer. And just as the royal box at Wimbledon, outwardly unremarkable, assumes for the crowd the aspect of a throne, the pool chairs in front of the gaudily painted bath structures were the focus for all eyes, arousing in those less fortunate the hope of one day crossing the artificial watery divide. This picture provokes my indignation. How false it is—how humorless you are in its midst! And yet, simultaneously, I experience another sensation, very like relief. Humiliation has been lifted from me. No matter how or why, you are a Success. Your cohorts defer to you; dapper mendicants in Brooks Brothers suits, awaiting your patronage. Your latest "revolutionary" idea was under discussion; the pros and cons of introducing split-size bottles for beer. The small amber glass vials were lined up like dumbbells along the flagstone border of the pool. The conferees—brewery executives, advertisers and salesmen—were gathered around a table with a gaily-striped, fringed umbrella at its center, their miens as grave as those of the scientists at Los Alamos. You basked in the sun, your face sanguine as your expectations, despite the fact that the California brewery was failing, draining the parent plant and forcing you to borrow heavily. Your prominent nose, your most exposed feature, was burned an explosive red, as though you willed the tropical heat to melt its detested contours. In New York you achieved a similar assault by sitting under a sunlight lamp at the Waldorf Astoria Hotel's barbershop. A seer, you were expounding your theories at length, your eyes closed against the glare, against possible opposition and against the thought of defeat. A telephone was brought out to you and you made a long distance call, oblivious to the rates. You harangued Armand de la Riviere in Paris, "This will really put Meistersinger on the map! The idea is even bigger than the beauty contest; an important breakthrough—"

At the other end of the line, in his Louis XV salon, Monsieur de la Riviere questioned his wildly enthusiastic associate in quiet tones. I recalled that trace of an accent that bespoke privilege rather than foreignness. Responding to your noisy vehemence, Armand de la Riviere's nose, sharp as a dagger, would be twitching uncontrollably, in disapproval. Or perhaps it was endorsement—but certainly he must be longing to hang up the telephone, to return to his more civilized business concerns.

The waiters circulated with preprandial cocktails, but you never drank. Eating was your one vice, and just as a child is pacified by his thumb, you took comfort in food. With the telephone propped beneath your chin, you reached greedily, with both hands, for the canapés, gulping avidly without chewing.

I shuddered. I had not forgotten an episode when a first date of mine made your acquaintance at table. I chattered in vain, to distract him from the sight of your gluttony; you, my humiliating secret, now exposed. And, just as before a crash, you grew to fabulous proportions when I caught my friend watching you shovel chocolate cake into the grotto of your mouth. I felt sure that he would depart, that he would not return.

But beside the pool at the hotel in California, the assembled corporation heads, film producers, scriptwriters, and most especially those on the opposite side, assure me that the pathetic schoolboy butt has been buried inside the pompous corpulence of the enviable man of affairs.

Your suite was the most deluxe in the hotel, but like all the rooms you inhabited, at home and on your travels, it had the disheveled aspect of a rag peddler's pushcart. Every inch of space was piled high with stacks of newspapers (you read four or five a day and absorbed their information like a computer), magazines, business reports, photographs of Miss Meistersinger contestants, illustrated catalogs of expensive foreign automobiles. In this rat's nest imposed upon your luxurious accommodations, you felt at ease. You lay on the bed, your stork's legs stretched out, your stockinged feet hanging over the edge. Like a gourmet with a cookbook you were perusing a Mercedes-Benz prospectus, while you waited for a masseur to knead your flesh in preparation for the evening.

Passing through the lobby you stopped, as usual,

at a newsstand to pick up the latest papers, before proceeding to the car rental concession: It was not that you were in need of transportation, a limousine and chauffeur were waiting for you at the front door under the Spanish porte-cochere. Your object was Ann Garrity, a young woman employed at this hotel showcase. Tonight you had purchased for her the offering of an oversized orchid, sinewy and tough, its purple petals like the beak of a macaw. But it was expensive, and, just as a knight encased in silver armor feels worthy of his ladylove, fortified by spending, you approached Ann Garrity. She had a pleasing appearance; tall, with rangy limbs, yet plump—her brown eyes were merry, her mouth generous and smiling, her nose satisfactorily small and snub. You moved cumbersomely toward her, weighted by heavy shoes with corrective plates in the soles (replacement for the iron braces), stooped, troubled already, although you had barely crossed forty, with high blood pressure and the onset of diabetes. Removed by the space of a continent, I can only imagine Ann Garrity as she accepts your gift, flattered by your attentions. But I am certain that you, like all romantics, had transformed the love object. The healthy, jolly girl had become a fragile princess, awaiting her rescuer in the captivity of the rental booth, beneath the neon-lighted pennant of Hertz automobiles. So Ann Garrity entered your history, where she was to play an important part as your third and last wife, the mother of Henrietta.

In remembering Ann, I hear first her voice: small,

light, childlike, a surprise issuing from her tall, broad-shouldered deep-bosomed body. But the potential for an outbreak of robust laughter, like a boisterous companion, hovered close by.

In summertime, when I drove past High Hill, at almost any hour of the day, through the openings in the hedges I could glimpse an abbreviated skirt fluttering like a white flag, waving above strong, suntanned, coltish legs: Ann playing tennis with ferocious energy and power, as though a devil were being exorcised!

You were proud of your wife's virile strength on the court, but your need to act the gallant protector to the helpless female was incorrigible.

"Baby Ann is so shy," you would say. "Do you know that when we were in England she wouldn't even meet her own cousin—a lord who lives in Sussex?"

Your bride had arrived at High Hill with a dowry of tenebrous oil paintings executed by her maternal British grandmother. They were portraits of Ann's mother, but the pigment was so thick (dark browns, muddy greens and rusty reds, the hue of dried blood) that it was necessary to look twice to distinguish the young girl and her posies from the pheasant, hanging head downward in one of those gloomy still-lifes that used to be part of the well-appointed Victorian dining room. You enjoyed showing off these proofs of your wife's British ancestry, her link to that remote lordly relative in Sussex. The Irish-American Mr. Garrity had died, but when Ann's mother arrived at High Hill for a visit, accompanied by one or another of her brood, the appearances of the football players, the Southern California housewives—Ann's siblings—indicated that Garrity genes had won out.

With the exception of the dark portraits, nothing was added to your home, nothing changed. Carmencita, the cocker spaniel, had been succeeded by Paws, a sheep dog, and there were three Persian kittens. In the playroom, "little girl" toys had replaced the boys' games of Sebastian Duke. The walls were decorated with ribbons and the shelves with silver trophies, won by Henrietta at the local horse shows. (A pony of her own would soon be lodged in a nearby stable.) You were always there, a towering landmark, standing behind the picket fence applauding your daughter as she, courageously, took the jumps—smart in her miniature crash helmet and fawn jodhpurs. After the show was over, she ran to you with her winnings. Your praise was lavish, your hugs strenuous, but you took no notice of the expression in her eyes, unprepared as you were to receive the gift of love, freely accorded.

In the pearl-gray oval dining room, you now instructed a docile but unresponsive "Baby Ann" in the setting of a table, in the manner of your mother. The water of the swimming pool was agitated again, and again you cautiously descended the terrace steps to watch the frolic.

You saw to it that life at High Hill should repeat itself. The round of habits was reassurance, sameness was the victory of your stubborn will over the violent disruptions of your past. Echoing in your own fashion our parents' special whistle (one short note, followed by two, followed by another more sustained single), to summon one another, though they might have been separated by no more than a single wall; on your return from the brewery you invariably called out, "Baby Ann, Baby Ann, I'm back. Where are you?"

In summer your only answer was the twang of ball meeting racket on the tennis court; in winter, your wife practiced indoors, in a prefabricated igloo beyond the range of your voice.

FIVE

FATHER WAS GROWING OLD. THE PURPLE POUCHES under his eyes were more pendulous and I suspected that the stylish cane he always carried had become a crutch rather than a man-about-town's accessory. He continued, however, to escort young women to restaurants, the theatre and concerts, while maintaining his customary silence on the subject of his private life. And just as a Victorian bed, rich in carvings, mute to the couplings to which it had been witness, stands out on the display floor among modern Castro convertibles, stripped, openly clinical in design, Father's secrecy contrasted with the frank discussions of sex endemic to the younger, psychologically-oriented generation. Words pertaining to sex rarely passed your lips either, Nicholas, but that was because of your prudishness and your chronic humility before women—something your father could never comprehend. Recently, he had been seeing Elsie Shay, an old friend from his bachelor days when she had been a Ziegfield Follies girl. Now she had the face of an aged, heavily powdered kitten and the vocabulary of a turn-of-the-century soubrette. "I haven't seen you in a coon's age!" she would exclaim, or "Let's sit down and have a cozy heart–to–gizzard." Father's loyalty to Elsie had persisted through the years, and he had helped her and her profligate husband, financially, finding jobs for her equally irresponsible sons; but during the time of his marriage, he stopped seeing her. Now—it was another sign of age—he summoned Elsie (a widow), pressing her into renewed service to him. She was as comfortable and available as the old carpet slippers he wore on his evenings at home. Through numerous signs, I was forced to concede that my parent was old. Yet you, Nicholas, refused to recognize this fact, although you fretted constantly about your inheritance. "You don't suppose that he might actually marry again?" you asked.

I was able to reassure you that there was nothing for you to fear on that score, nothing would be altered in Father's will. But, for the most part, you were cheerful and oblivious, confident that your father, too, would never die.

Father, nearing eighty, never missed a day at the brewery. Each morning, the faithful Kevin would drive him along the same route to Bushwick. Fearing that our time together was limited, my hold on him pried loose by the passing of the years, I would sometimes ask to accompany him to Brooklyn. Relics from the past had become interesting to me: a sign of age as sure as the pouches beneath my father's eyes. Until recently, I had avoided reminiscences, now I begged for the facts and anecdotes that Father could relate. And, just as a child on a beach picks up and treasures ordinary shells and pebbles, remembered bits of family history, details of life inside the brewery compound, in my imagination, took on a patina, mother-of-pearl, rosy, pleasingly fluted, aromatic from the sea of the past.

I was unable, however, to share Father's pleasure in the sights we passed along the way. Through the window of his automobile, he would point out the hideous housing developments. Stoop for stoop, unindividuated, with front doors newly and garishly painted red, green, blue and yellow, yards the size of postage stamps, they were built close to one another, yet they appeared desolate in their very crowdedness. Father surveyed them with the satisfaction of a feudal landlord reviewing the tapestried landscape, the fields and farms of his domain, saying in praise of modern engineering, "Do you realize that only a few years ago there was nothing here but waste—swampland?"

I was unable to join him either, when he attempted to talk with me about my mother; my sense of loss and shock at her sudden death had abated so little after all this time that at the mention of her I still froze like a deer startled by the blinding glare of headlights. I envied you, Nicholas, for the volubility of your sentiments; you could relieve Father's loneliness, while I abandoned him on the small, dwindling memory of the island of his marriage.

At his office, he was joined by his brother, Charles, who still sat facing him at their old-fashioned, double rolltop desk. In this place, Uncle Charles assumed for me the value of an heirloom. His beard sparser, his blue eyes paler, he nonetheless reinforced my recollection of my grandfather. I was, however, unable to discern the same strain in the portrait of our great-grandfather, the founder, Joseph Bloch, who looked dour, with small black eyes under bushy brows. Only the heavy gold chain spanning his somber waistcoat linked him to Karl, my grandfather, and Charles, my uncle.

As far back as I can recall, I have been attracted by dynastic continuity. As a child, I wallowed in romantic adventures by Alexandre Dumas that took place against the background of the outrageous magnificence of the French monarchy. At Buckingham Palace, I peered over the tall black fur helmets of the guards and through the openings of the iron grillwork wall, in order to catch a single glimpse, always denied me, of King George VI and Queen Elizabeth. Once, upon leaving Blenheim Castle on "visitor's day," footsore from trudging over great reaches of marble floors, I caught sight at the rear of the mansion of a clothesline with laundry flapping in the summer breeze. Nearby a young woman wheeled a perambulator. This homely vision was more interesting, by far, than roped-off gilded furniture, richly paneled walls and marble mosaic floors. Modestly tucked away, the domestic scene resounded like a royal procession heralding the arrival of yet another generation in the long line of a noble family. Inside an ordinary baby carriage, not intended for public view, resided flesh-and-blood proof that history was alive.

My preoccupation was not always snobbish. It did not depend on titles, nor was it necessary that my show pieces dwell in palaces and aristocratic mansions. A crude potter's shop in Oberammergau had served the same purpose. In our early childhood, Father, influenced by his Germanic upbringing, liked to travel with his family to the land of his forebears, where Joseph Bloch had founded the brewery in the early part of the eighteenth century. As soon as we arrived in Germany, you, Nicholas, were able to spout the language. Was it a mysterious atavistic gene that gave you this power, or merely your nimble tongue and prodigious memory? Our parents declared your accent perfect. But I squirmed at your loud show-off speeches addressed to headwaiters and taxi drivers. To me you were merely a clown in ill-fitting, borrowed clothes. But I, too, felt at home in Germany. I admired the quaint, gabled, gingerbread style houses of the cities, the neatly cultivated countryside, the dark forests and gentle green slopes of the mountains of Bavaria.

Oberammergau was known as the setting for the Passion Play, performed there since the Middle Ages by its native citizens. At regular intervals, the story of the Crucifixion was enacted, its theatricality heightened by the introduction of demons spawned by the fancy of generations of darkness. The protagonist, the figure of Christ, mild and martyred, destined to be pinned to his Cross, was an old acquaintance often encountered in the paintings on the walls of museums. I had also met him inside the hushed, clammy-cold, prismatic semi-night of ancient cathedrals. Hortense, our French maid, a Catholic, had told me that He died to save us and that He was the Son of God. Of the role of Jews in this drama, Hortense made no mention. Did she even realize that her "patrons" were "Israelites"? Or, having served our family for so long, did her devotion tend to elevate us to a position of honorific immunity that set us apart, allowing us to overcome our own origins? I had never actually witnessed a Passion Play, but I had seen pictures of former performances and had noticed that the demons always looked the same: dark, with large false noses— caricatures of the type our parents described as "looking Jewish." This coincidence made no impression on me. I was ignorant of Jewish history, culture and religion. For a short period, under the supervision of a private teacher, I had pasted meaningless illustrations of biblical stories in a school notebook. But, as I had not read the Old Testament, entered a synagogue, or met a rabbi, this foolish occupation ended and its meager teachings were forgotten. And the only picture that remained in memory was that of Samson with his long, wild, sinewy locks, which I knew contained his strength. On the subject of Semites, our parents uttered as little as possible. But it was said that the Passion Play, a traditional people's art form, was universal and, therefore, belonged to everyone.

Sightseeing with Father was always a delight. Hand in hand, he and I had visited the pottery shop belonging to Anton Lang, the current portrayer of the Savior. On this day, he was merely a simple craftsman who greeted us with cordiality and introduced us to his son, who might soon inherit the role from him. So the march from generation to generation would be unbroken: a solid phalanx at ease in their dual roles of citizen and actor, a succession extending all the way back to the Middle Ages. I examined the two men, so strikingly alike, with ruddy complexions and fair beards, both dressed in coarse work aprons. When we left, Anton Lang presented me with a pottery bowl as a souvenir of Oberammergau, where I never went again. Neither Father nor I could imagine that the very hand that tended the furnace in the rustic potter's shed would, perhaps, a few years later feed the crematoriums of Auschwitz, Maidanek or Bergen-Belsen.

In the presence of my father and uncle seated before their desks at the brewery, recalling my grandfather who had been there before them, I conjured up my own truncated dynasty, starting at Ludwigsburg. Then a door opened and a shaft of neon light from your adjacent office, Nicholas, caused the oak-paneled walls and old brown leather furniture of your elders' place of work suddenly to appear worn, shabby and unsubstantial. You stood for a moment on the threshold between the two rooms and your hulking form seemed to dwarf your father and uncle, the guardians of my past, my wishful dreams were scattered.

We celebrated Father's eighty-fifth birthday with a family gathering. After dinner we sat on the terrace of our home, spectators, again, to the sameness and the variations of the celestial kaleidoscope spread before us at day's end. And, just as a solitary traveler in a foreign land welcomes a touch of home— a familiar bend in the road, a similar four-poster bed in a hotel room—that tells him, "You have not gone so far away, after all," I watched the return of sunset and derived from it a sense of permanence.

Nicholas, you were galvanized that evening, talking, shouting without cease, drowning out the rest of us with your loud braying. And I felt mounting within me my recurrent rage at your insensitivity. And, as in my childhood, it rendered me silent, the old questions exploding in my mind: Where did you spring from? How was it possible for you to be my brother, my father's son, my mother's? How would I manage to ignore the shameful burden of your presence? As always, you were blandly unaware of my sullen retreat, my glances of disgust, and I was included in your cheerful amiable reach: you were still blind to others, deaf to the detonations of your own bombardings.

"It's the best buy on the market," you were saying to Father who was protesting your wildly extravagant gift of a new limousine. "It's a beauty! Did you notice the upholstery? I can have your monogram put on the door without extra charge. . . ."

Yes, I thought sarcastically, a coat of arms; just like your prep-school blazer with the escutcheon on the pocket proclaiming ersatz social status.

"The old car ran perfectly well. Your spending will ruin us all," Father answered, and he admired the modest birthday gifts proffered by the rest of his family: Ann, your wife, your daughter, Henrietta, grown into a chubby pre-adolescent with the promise of future prettiness, my husband, my son on whom Father's eyes rested with warmth and approbation. But even as the battle raged between you, his regard for you, Nicholas, his son, was special, compounded of exasperation, need and a love transcending personal judgment—archetypal, legendary. You were Joseph to his Jacob, Absalom to his David. I can hear Father now, scoffing at these fanciful musings of mine, at my foolishness in comparing his pragmatic, down-to-earth way of life to those archaic fairy tales.

But on the night of his eighty-fifth birthday, such notions were far away. I looked at Father and felt a clutch of helpless panic at my entrails. He was going to die. I noticed that his skin was yellow, without the pink-brown glow of health I was used to; his body was shrunken. There was a skeleton, jaunty in my father's clothes; his white pin-striped summer flannels, his butterfly foulard bow tie. And this apparition presided at the feast, usurping the place of honor. The celebration was a travesty for everyone; only Father knew nothing. And you— you invariably refused to confront your fears. Today, so many years later, I can still see you sprawled, larger than life on our terrace, your red sunburned face lit by the setting sun. You were attempting tirelessly to soften another opponent, but this adversary was not to be shouted into submission, nor would he listen to your bargaining or accept your bribes.

Not long before, on a hot July day, the kindly

half-Jewish German refugee doctor, who regularly had appeared during the winter at Father's Sunday luncheons, summoned me to his office. Dr. Elias Steinmetz was no more, he had died like any ordinary mortal. The glossy, penetrating black eyes had vanished from my existence forever. But my dependence on him had dwindled in recent years, as well as the faith he had been empowered to evoke. Father and I attended his funeral, but since Dr. Steinmetz had made it a rule never to be present at the burial of a patient (was each death, perhaps, a personal failure, a blow to his ego?), I sat in the funeral parlor in body only, experiencing no emotion during the meaningless, non-denominational rites. One does not bury a god, even a false one. Father also appeared unmoved. I had noted that, in his old age, the demise of a contemporary did not evoke sadness but rather, a somewhat cocky sense of victory. At breakfast Father would turn to the obituary page of the morning newspaper first, and while relishing his stewed prunes with cream, he would read out loud the name of some acquaintance,

"So Adolf Lerman is dead! And only seventy-five!"

In the doctor's waiting room I examined minutely the arrangements of wildflowers brought from his country home upstate, so reminiscent of the hills of his native Bavaria, to which he had never returned. The patients, like the doctor, were mostly refugees, and when the door of the inner sanctum opened, the doctor himself appeared and bid them, one by one, to enter. He addressed them in German and it sounded chummy and cordial, as though he were inviting them into a pre-war Munich beer hall. But when my turn came, his accented English had the grave ring of the summons from a judge of the highest court. And, just as in classical art, the female form of Justice is represented holding, in each hand, her scales, the doctor's stubby figure seemed to be balancing the weightier matter of life and death.

I sat in the office separated by the wide desk, and again examined those curiously fragile wildflowers, lined up along the windowsill in a simulated rock garden. In the glare and throbbing heat emanating from Park Avenue, the blooms hung their wilting heads. The doctor was saying, "Your father's X-rays show a definite shadow on the lung. It is cancer, unmistakably."

He toyed with a pencil, drawing senseless doodles upon his prescription pad, as though to illustrate his shocking disclosure. "Of course, at your father's age, growth will be slow; it may even go on for several years more. But rest assured; I will see to it that he will not suffer."

On the street beyond the window, sunlight and the noise of traffic exploded. Incredibly, the world would spin on without Father. The office was a tomb.

"I think it best not to tell the patient about the findings. Let him enjoy, as much as possible, what is left to him of life."

The doctor's words were benign but, oddly, they seemed to be formulated by only half of his mouth, the other part, bisected by the Heidelberg dueling scar, remained immobile. I had always viewed the wound as romantic, a remnant of the old regime— and enviable, too, as a sign of Aryan lineage. Now it seemed to divide Jew from Gentile, splitting the good doctor in sinister fashion.

"Above all," he continued, "we must take care of your father at home. For this I need your co-operation. Your brother will want to try everything, he will leave no stone unturned—and it will be useless. It will only cause unnecessary suffering."

So at this hour, too, I gathered my forces to oppose you. "Have you told Nicholas yet?"

"No. All in good time, all in good time. We will manage together."

The doctor stood up, the interview was over. At the door, he grasped my hand warmly, but I dared not look into his face, where that mouth slashed by the jagged scar conveyed contradictory messages of consolation and cruelty.

Two years passed and Father's birthdays rolled around. Now there was no family group on the terrace, no sunset to draw the attention upward to absorb the chatter as it did the insignificant squeakings and croakings of the invisible short-lived summer insects. Father lay in bed in his New York City apartment. He had suffered another of those disabling bouts of illness, each supposed to be the last. Yet he would rise again, throw back his shoulders and, armored in his long john underwear (worn at all seasons), his dark business suit girded by the old-fashioned gold watch chain spanning his vest, he returned to the brewery, to his double rolltop desk. He occupied it alone now; Uncle Charles had died two years before.

Summers presented a problem for Father, the trips to Europe were no longer possible. In recent times Elsie Shay had been his traveling companion, a willing but saucy slave who snuggled catlike into the comfort of their hotel suites, uncomplaining about the numerous, last-minute changes of plan. Now Father was confined to New York City and its suburbs. He had once before spent a summer in Westchester with you, Nicholas, after your divorce from Margo and before your discovery of Ramona Randall. You and he had played bachelor hosts in a palatial rented house. Whenever I see flourishing rhododendron bushes, in my mind's eye that tall white edifice rises above them like a luxury cruise ship anchored alongside a forest of glossy green foliage. The interior was impressive in English-manor style. Like yours, Father's taste ran to the grandiose. During her lifetime, my mother's simplicity acted as a mild restraint; she found the Villa d'Esté on Lake Como malarial, the marble halls of the palace hotel chill and depressing, while for Father it did more for his spirits than for his health, the medicinal spa waters of Karlsbad.

The rented house boasted many reception rooms hung with ancestral portraits. On the stair landing, the deceased wife of the "swell" who owned the estate was painted in a scarlet ball gown. A beautiful brunette, she looked down with haughty dark eyes at the interlopers below.

Newly arrived from the city, sweaty in your crumpled suit, your arms full of the magazines, newspapers, advertising proposals, you would stand worshipfully before the painting. Forgiving and forgetful of the circumstances of your abandonment, you would exclaim to any listener, "Doesn't she look exactly like Little Miss Margo?"

Thus in your fancy you identified yourself and your single state with the aristocratic widower, your landlord.

Despite the extravagance he had once shared with you, Father and Ann, your wife, were joined now in their efforts to stem the flow of your spending. Although I was unaware of it, Father was being drained by his compliance to your demands through the years. The brewery, too, was beginning to totter, but in response to Father's warnings, you would repeat, "One must move forward no matter what the cost! Soon Meistersinger will be number one nationally. We have been local much too long!"

In the ground floor guest room at High Hill, shaded at every hour of the day a dark bottle-green by the trees that pressed close to the windows, Father brooded. He was like an ancient gardener trapped inside his own hothouse, strangled by a monster plant of his own creating. He seemed, however, scarcely more contented at my home. Our roles reversed, he was too proud to accept my care, my anxiety and my ill-concealed sadness. With the faithful Kevin, whose broad ruddy face shone with good nature, even his rimless spectacles glinted kindliness, Father would flee back to the torrid city, to his own apartment where he was better able to resume the role of protective parent. When I visited him there, before I took my departure, he would reach into his trouser pocket for loose change, and producing a coin, he would say, "Here, daughter, is your carfare to go home," just as when I was a child he had provided the money for my weekly allowance.

Sometimes in the evening the good doctor came to call, as a friend, to enjoy a refreshing glass of golden Meistersinger beer. The doctor often brought a bouquet of those fragile field flowers from his rustic retreat. But Father brushed them brusquely, almost rudely, aside and chose, also, to ignore the scrutiny of the doctor's eyes while they chatted together of trivial matters.

On his eighty-seventh birthday, Father lay in bed, too weak to perform any act of self-assertion. Nicholas, you had been away on another business trip. But you were expected momentarily, and when the door opened to admit you, Father's sickroom, blinds down against the heat, was suddenly illumined by the flickering light of eighty-seven tiny candles crowded upon the wide circumference of a gigantic birthday cake. You advanced cautiously, clumsily, in the manner with which you descended the steps to your swimming pool, lustily singing, "Happy Birthday to you, happy birthday, dear Father—"

Your face in the wavering light was actually beaming. Drunk on your own high spirits, like a salesman at a convention, you carefully placed the cake on the night table, routing the unavailing battalion of medicine bottles. The pink-and-white icing, the miniature flames, the sugary inscription, lettered with a flourish amid the candy rosebuds transported me back to the parties of our childhood.

I saw you seated at the head of a table, party hat gaily askew on your curly head. But you were cringing with fear at the firecrackers exploding around you. You would not touch the frilly paper cannons and you covered your ears with your hands. Your guests, your persecutors from the schoolyard, had called a temporary truce in order to enjoy the festivities, presents and sweets. The ruffians were even hushed for an instant, at the climax, the entrance of the cake in all its ritual solemnity.

"Blow out the candles, Nicholas," they chanted, "and you will get your wish!"

You inhaled mightily, your cheeks inflated like the illustrations of the Four Winds in our picture books, and then exhaled, extinguishing all the flames at once.

Everyone around the table applauded. But I remembered that tomorrow was another school day: What form of torture would it bring you? What were you wishing, Nicholas? Did you pray that you might be rid of your tormentors forever? Perhaps the role of butt had become so habitual that you accepted it, taking it for granted like the air you breathed— in and out in explosive effort—causing all the candles to go dark. . . . But I, seated as far from you as possible, vowed that there would come a day when I would no longer be witness to your humiliations. Then, as later, I tried to sever the sibling connection between us with the sharpened blade of my contempt.

"Blow out the candles, Father," you commanded, ignoring the invalid in his bed, with barely enough breath left to continue existing.

Not waiting for Father to respond, you puffed at the eighty-seven candles yourself. But one resisted you; quickly, almost furtively, you put it out also.

"What's all this nonsense?" Father grumbled. But his face was transformed. Against his better judgment, hope kindled his eyes. Soon you and he were launched on another business argument as though you were seated across the conference table at the brewery.

All the while you were removing the candles from the cake. "The first piece goes to the birthday boy," you said, "It's chocolate"—your only addiction—"all the way through."

But Father was not listening. He had swung his legs, twig-thin, protruding from his white cotton nightdress, out of bed, and was preparing to rise to his feet. Tomorrow he would be back at work.

Unexpectedly, I was invaded by a wave of gratitude to you, Nicholas. Your blind refusal to accept the fact of Father's condition, his nearness to death, was more tonic than all the doctor's palliatives. Holy idiot, idiot *savant*, you had performed a miracle!

SIX

OUR LIVES COINCIDED LESS AND LESS FREQUENTLY
after Father's death. Yet for some reason you never
disappeared altogether from the horizon of my consciousness. Although I no longer visited the brewery, I thought of you at the helm, without Father's
support, a wildly erratic captain lacking his first
mate. Now that Father and Uncle Charles were gone,
Dr. Helmuth Schneider moved into their office, adjacent to yours—a German tutor, keeping a censorious watch on a wayward pupil. Yet in the
presence of René, young scion of the de la Rivieres,
Dr. Schneider became obsequious, deferentially
rubbing his pudgy hands together, his blue eyes
heavier than ever with the weight of his respect.
René, representing the majority stockholders, was
technically in financial control of the brewery; but,
like a black gossamer-winged butterfly strayed from
the elegance of the Parc Monceau into the uncon-
genial, coarse marketplace atmosphere of Les Halles,
his appearances in Bushwick were rare and you
were left in charge, without superiors.

It was your pleasant duty to report once a year

to the senior Armand de la Riviere in Paris. Although it is certain that he had received unfavorable accounts of your mismanagement from Dr. Schneider, the Meistersinger brewery was too small an enterprise to focus Armand de la Riviere's twitchy attention. He was older and more burdened than ever by his swelling fortune, his holdings in many nations; the brewery, your universe, was no more to him than a suitable kindergarten where his heir might learn the ABC's of business. In Paris you would find yourself dining at the de la Rivieres', seated between a *duchesse* and a *marquise*, a situation more intoxicating than the vintage wines poured from ancient, musty bottles into heirloom cut-crystal goblets. You were in your element, surrounded by old titles, fortunes, old and new, regarded, yourself, by the company as a millionaire from America. The only Jew present, you felt that at last you had penetrated "inside."

Long ago, when we were still living at Green Meadows, you and I had stood side by side, pressed against the fence enclosing the riding ring where the local horse show took place. Wistfully, we had watched the others, children of our own age (the offspring of county families, members of the "hunt" and clubs to which our parents did not belong), clearing the barriers, coattails flying like pennants, crash helmets, crowns upon their heads. We were united in exclusion, both of us a little in love with the victors as they trotted smartly off with their blue ribbons and trophies.

After Paris you returned to Bushwick, proud of your success abroad. At the de la Rivieres'—"my partners"—you had cleared the social jumps and you rolled the noble titles on your tongue using your showiest French. Thus fortified, despite the financial precariousness of your situation, you were more optimistic than ever, oblivious to the approaching end.

For the Bloch family, distaff side as well as male, identification was closely linked to the Meistersinger Brewery. As a small child I was aware of the pride my relatives took in their solid, burgher achievement. You and I had learned to recognize the big yellow trucks and, inwardly, we saluted the familiar *Meistersinger Beer* insignia emblazoned on their sides in German lettering. Our loyalty was as deep as and more intimate than when we stood before the American flag or listened to the national anthem.

So it was surprising that, years later, the Meistersinger Brewery passed out of my life with so little impact. But you, Nicholas, waged a mighty battle and when you were defeated your grief was inconsolable, as at the demise of a beloved kinsman. Remote from the scene of battle, with only scraps of information to go on, I constructed a melodrama. René, now grown into a stage villain, was costumed as a dashing *boulevardier*. Bored with his humdrum post at the brewery, he spread his dark wings, the folds of a black opera cape, and flew back to Paris where he belonged. He notified his father of his intention to quit, and Armand, before installing another representative in his son's place, reviewed the financial status of the business, focusing, at last, on the deplorable figures. He decided to put an end to it, to sell Meistersinger to the highest bidder. You, a pitiful, beleaguered Punch, fought the move with all your might. Having no weapon to brandish, you defended yourself with promises: the failed California plant would go, your advertising budget would be cut drastically. On your very life you vowed that henceforth you would be frugal, would economize on all sides. You fell to your knees, a broken puppet, pleading. But the enemy was ice-cold toward all entreaties. Those who had plotted against you, the family members of the board of directors, headed by a hops heiress, swarthy and thin as a charred bone—once the loudest voice in favor of your ouster—in a reversal of her role, sided with you in this theatre of dissolution. Seated around the conference table, in the old residence, the family shrilly protested the sale, while the stern portrait of their founder-ancestor looked on mutely. But it was all to no avail, the de la Rivieres held the majority vote and the brewery was sold. Our enterprise, our history, its dimming genesis in mythological eighteenth-century Ludwigsburg, was no more.

I thought of Father. He had believed that he could make your position secure by rendering the rest of the family impuissant, and he had introduced the de la Rivieres, into the brewery compound. Father, pragmatic, independent, energetic, resourceful— my support and reassurance; is it possible that he had the vulnerability of those with willfully limited vision? At any rate, he was unable to control your destiny from the grave.

So it came about that in middle age, broken in health, bankrupt, your public images ("beer tycoon," "brilliant creator of Miss Meistersinger," "advertising genius") exploded like balloons, you nakedly faced the future. Beset by debts on all sides, ignoring your wife, "Baby Ann's," implorings, you refused to sell High Hill, the setting for your many domestic upheavals. Like an infant with his security blanket, you clung to the comfort of its worn endurance.

You had telephoned before arriving that Sunday morning. Despite your troubles, your voice had sounded cheerful, friendly. My husband awaited your appearance with stony contempt, and I was in the usual state of nervous embarrassment that always went with the exhibition of you, Nicholas, my brother, before others. To allay my unease I even reviewed the praise you had received from strangers. Recently I had met an acquaintance among a gathering of friends, an Austrian countess married to a wealthy American painter. A Catholic, she had seven children and had also found the time to write and publish several books of abstract ecclesiastical philosophy while remaining as frivolously pretty as a porcelain Dresden shepherdess. She had startled me by saying, "I met your brother the other evening. What a charming man, and so brilliant."

I stared at her in disbelief; but just as someone preserves four–leaf clovers pressed inside the covers of a family album, I conserved the compliment with a few others. Some consoling, compensating memory pictures of you I kept also: emperor, in your director's chair at the coronation of the first Miss Meistersinger, or lounging on the prestigious side of the Beverly Hills Hotel pool, the object of admiration from across the artificial blue water. But it was no use. As I waited for your unexpected visit, not knowing what was coming, I felt like someone who for a long time has been at pains to conceal a physical deformity, and was now about to have it exposed. The sound of the wheels of your car on the gravel driveway announced your arrival. You walked through the house to join us on the lawn, tripping over the threshold. I was shocked by your appearance; enormously fat a short time before, you had become so thin that your silhouette reminded me of the gangling schoolboy of long ago. On closer inspection, you looked ill, and those perfectly matched, oval teeth, were lustrous pearls in your wasted face.

You inquired with warm avuncular interest about our son, whom you had not seen for years. You bragged about Henrietta, your daughter. "She is a wonderful little rider. For her tenth birthday, I gave her a horse and now she wins all the blue ribbons. You must come swimming in our pool and see her swan dives and jack knives. And Henrietta is pretty as a picture—"

On and on—until I began to think that you had nothing special to say, after all. But you were wearing your Wellington School blazer, always a sign of an important occasion. The blow fell, my hunchback, my clubfoot were in full sight! Without any alteration in your chatty tone, you turned to my husband, saying, "The fact is, at this moment, I am broke. I cannot pay my debts, I may even have to take Henrietta out of private school. Could you lend me twenty-five thousand dollars? It's only temporary, of course. I have several leads for a big job at top salary. You will be paid with interest, I guarantee—"

My husband quickly acquiesced, although he knew the money would never be returned. His generosity was more humiliating than a refusal. Anything to be rid of you as soon as possible!

Your response was effusive, sycophantic. I winced, no, no, you were not a brother.

"A million thanks! You will never regret this, I swear . . ." You prepared to go. "I'm sorry I can't stay longer. Henrietta is waiting for me to take her to church."

In my mind's eye, I followed you. The smell of incense, the prismatic rays from stained glass, the Crucifix, the holy stoup bringing back the peek inside you had had on that wintry street long ago, while we waited to go home where the door would open upon the magnificence of the tree on Christmas Eve. I imagined you walking down the aisle, unnaturally tall, with the small, fair girl by your side. Her confiding hand in yours was warmth. Did you hope that, camouflaged in the borrowed raiment of your faith, the most insignificant supplicant in the house of worship of the historical enemy of the Jews, there would be no more to fear? God would listen to your prayers, too?

"You are both great!" you were exclaiming. "You

will never be sorry you did this. I always tell everybody how close we are!"

I clenched my teeth and avoided my husband's eye.

In your relief, you seemed to swell, to fill out the clothes that had hung limply from your diminished body at the time of your arrival. But before you turned, in the bright sunlight, I noticed that the Wellington School coat of arms on the pocket of your blazer was tarnished, torn, the golden threads hanging loose like disconnected wires.

During the following months you kept us informed about your ups and downs in the job market. I received hysterical calls: you were going to be president of this, chairman or director of that; but all the time you were unemployed, your beloved brewery off limits, in the hands of strangers. Finally you found a modest position in a large advertising firm. "The chances of getting to the top are very good," you told me when you announced your victory. "After all, Miss Meistersinger *was* the biggest promotional idea of our era, and my connections through the Brewers' Association are sure to bring in many accounts."

I was accustomed to your hopeful boastings, your exaggerations, and I was dubious about your grand predictions for the future. I did, however, obliquely admire the determination that permitted you to seek, without complaint (in middle age, the former chief of Meistersinger Brewery), a place no more prestigious than that offered to a young hopeful newly graduated from college. For this reason, shortly after you had started to work for Brandt and Hogan, we reluctantly accepted your invitation to dinner to meet "my bosses."

The changes at High Hill were subtle: one had to look hard to notice the frayed chintz pillow on the sofa, the worn pile in the carpet. At a quick glance, it was still a gracious, affluent home, with its wide curving staircase, its oval oyster shell–gray dining room and the many stately French doors opening onto the terrace with the pool and tennis court below. A new generation of pets—poodle and Persian cat—had succeeded the old. On the living room wall hung a portrait you had commissioned: Rose Red and Snow White, your wife and daughter, a wholesome mother-child pair, worthy of any advertisement for a skin conditioner or breakfast cereal.

You received us, the genial host, your wiry hair slicked down, pomaded, as when your private barber and masseur had visited the house. You introduced James Hogan, the company president, thin, with thin lips, thinning hair, wearing a narrow knitted black string tie. Your manner was deferential, humble. It was shocking to realize that only yesterday you had been sitting behind your own executive's desk, loud and overbearing, issuing commands while chiefs like James Hogan wooed you. That evening the "artists" and "writers" from the company had been invited also. You showed especial admiration for these Cézannes and Thomas Manns of the world of marketing. The advertising jargon had always been familiar to you. I, too, knew that "creative artists" meant copywriters and layout specialists. Did I only imagine that during this evening at High Hill the executives and their wives regarded you with sarcastic curiosity? That in their midst you were again the outsider suing for entry? Only one person seemed genuinely well disposed toward you: Chip Middlemarch, handsome, broad-shouldered, resembling a Greek discus thrower, with close-cropped curly hair like a copper helmet. You moved among the guests, impervious to nuances, happy to be entertaining your new associates at High Hill.

Ann played her part shyly. She wore her long hostess skirt like a costume. It concealed her legs, still youthful and coltish, though her body had thickened and squint lines had appeared around her laughing brown eyes. You were proud of your wife, and the apricot poodle, the fluffy Persian cat. On the terrace the dying sun showed up the peeling white paint on the wrought-iron furniture and railing.

"Baby Ann, will you please pass the canapés to Mr. Hogan," you said.

Did Ann wince at the ridiculous name—or did she not even hear it anymore?

"So, you are Nick's sister," Mr. Hogan was saying to me. "You must have been delighted to know all those real American beauties, the Miss Meistersinger girls. Whatever became of Jill Boyd, queen of them all?"

At this point you interrupted with an enthusiastic, verbose monologue, rescuing me from Mr. Hogan's attention and his pale, fishy eyes. I had an uncomfortable feeling you had confronted this company before. But now, Nicholas, your wallet and pockets were empty; like an animal, defenseless, lacking fangs and claws, you moved through the jungle ignorant of your danger.

"Wait for me," you called, your voice plaintive, distant, muffled, lost among the great dark trees and the twisting paths, indistinct in the night. We (Ann, my husband and I) marched ahead, while you, your gait uncertain, hesitant over the partly buried tangle of roots along the way, struggled to reach us, repeating that faraway wail, "Wait for me . . . wait for me . . ."

You had asked us to this out-of-doors concert and it was a rare occasion that found the four of us together. The symphony orchestra and the famous pianist were performing at Primavera, a music center in northern Westchester that had once been a private estate. I recalled the owners, from my childhood, chiefly because of a recital I had attended in New York City, during which the mistress of Primavera played an electrical instrument—defunct, I believe, today—intricate, with plugs, wires, push buttons and automatic pedals; but the notes seemed to issue, magically, from the wild strands of her bushy hair, more alive than her fragile body and her pale face with its delicate features. And, just as a lily surprises us by its graceful form and acrid odor, it was startling to hear those weird barnyard squawks emerging from the *art nouveau* beauty of the performer. Her proud husband sat in a first-tier box. His money had made the concert possible. Husband and wife had long been dead and this public music festival was dedicated in their memory.

At Primavera the musicians played on a dais beneath a band shell, but the rows of seats were in the open, surrounded by the summer-sweet smells of garden flowers, more pungent because unseen, their delicate shapes and colors blotted out by the theatrical lights of the alfresco concert hall. On this night the program opened with a composition by a renowned modern Russian. With the first strains I experienced a sensation of déjà vu: the present scene was penetrated by an event from the past, so real that I felt the adult casing of my body melting away; Ann and my husband faded from existence. Only you, Nicholas, two seats removed from me, were there. . . .

You were dressed in your best summer suit and your face still bore traces of its early Little Lord Fauntleroy prettiness. We had been scrubbed and combed and bedecked in our finest clothes for the festivity: the Thalheims were giving an out-of-doors ballet presentation, introducing to the United States a dance troupe already famous in France. The viewers were select; as next-door neighbors, we were all invited, even you and I, Nicholas. I was wearing my best party dress, white crepe de chine with net ruffles, sashed in pale blue taffeta, and the "daisy chain," brought out only on grand occasions. This fragile object had totem value for me. When the hair-fine chain with its three pendant tiny enamel daisies was placed around my neck, I was aware of my own dignity, like an infant princess. My mother had worn the necklace at the same age, so I became the inheritor of the past, the fading storybook unreality of my mother as a girl. The Thalheim property looked altered in the darkness. I recognized none of the landmarks from my daytime walks with *Fräulein*. Because they were also children (like little boys and girls eyeing one another in the lobby of a foreign hotel), I felt an unaccustomed bond with the youngest generation of the Thalheim clan, who were also curried and beautified for the occasion. The audience sat, uncomfortably, on hard, folding chairs, beneath Japanese lanterns strung between the trees. One of the sons, the instigator of this importation, stepped before the curtain of the improvised stage to give a brief history of the ballet company, of its émigré White Russian director, as well as of the Russian composer of the opening piece. Paul Thalheim's speech was jerky, in his excitement and enthusiasm he almost stammered. But the audience was already twisting restlessly on the hard chairs. The orchestra began to play the overture, the curtain rose and, in formal patterns, the ballerinas drifted on stage. All alike, with long legs and arms, and small neat heads, not so much human as the flawless representation of music made material. . . .

Years later at the symphony concert at Primavera, transported by that same music, I had the impulse, Nicholas, to reach out to touch you. "Are you back there with me?" I wanted to ask. You, too, had been at that faraway place. We had shared. . . .

Following that evening at the Thalheims,' from adult conversations I gathered that the presentation had been a failure. The Russian ballet director, worshipped today, and the equally admired composer were not popular at first. Audiences exposed to the cerebral, ponderous innovations of modern dance, accustomed to the overpowering emotionalism of Wagner, declared the music "cold" and ballet "obsolete," leftover from the court of the czars. Even my mother, herself a musician, an avid listener with receptive antennae, had been unmoved. The youngest Thalheim son was considered an eccentric. Instead of concerning himself with the dance, why was he not following a suitable career—law or banking? The future, unlike the past, cannot infiltrate the present, but must remain hidden, unpredictable. And the guests at the Thalheims' would have been very surprised to see the passionate devotees today lining up to see and hear what they had spurned that night long ago.

The *maestro* at Primavera was taking his bows, beckoning the members of his orchestra to stand and acknowledge with him the enthusiastic applause. The spell was broken. During the intermission only you, Nicholas, insisted upon visiting the buffet. We wandered off, leaving you at the long table, clutching a piece of pastry in one hand, a glass of ginger ale in the other. You called out again in that pleading tone swallowed up by darkness, "Wait for me, wait for me!" like a child afraid of the dark.

Your voice was an undertow pulling me back into the shallows of our past.

"Wait for me, wait for me!" I did not heed you, nor did I even ask if you, too, remembered.

PART 3

THE WEAKEST LINK

ANN'S VOICE ON THE TELEPHONE, CHILDLIKE, breathless, always surprisingly light issuing from so robust a person, was an inappropriate harbinger for the message she was about to deliver. "Nicholas has had a massive stroke," she said. "It happened at the post office where he had gone to mail Margo's alimony. It's very bad—there was no warning. Of course, he was always too scared to see a doctor about his high blood pressure . . ." The account trailed off, the hint of laughter usually lurking behind Ann's speech had turned into a suppressed wail. Like someone with faulty vision who attempts to decipher a blurred page, I was unable, at first, to absorb the news. But during the instant of silence, the fog of incomprehension lifted and, as though I had been present, I saw my brother sprawled on the stone floor of the post office. In one useless hand he was still clutching the envelope containing the punishing, crushing alimony check.

Although awareness of life's fragility is always with us, when illness and death strike we are startled by the cruel unnaturalness of the event, and we forget altogether that it is the expected, inevitable consequence of living. In order to endure my proximity to the nightmare of Nicholas's plight, I built many protective barriers of habit—anodynes of repetition. The road to the hospital invariably veered to the left, up an incline where a traffic light blinked; with relief and recognition I drove by a shopping mall, and the Woolworth sign never failed to hail me as I passed. Yet when the great prison-like edifice of the hospital loomed into view, these wayside totems lost their power and my heart pounded in anticipation of the dreaded visit. Nicholas lay on his bed, barely alive, motionless, a mechanical man functioning only through wires and tubes. He was attended by lunar creatures in white who refused to respond to my questions. Just when it seemed this stasis would continue forever, it ended: improvement was detected. Although Nicholas, the irrepressible talker, remained mute, he managed triumphantly, to wiggle a toe! Mobility was returning to one arm and understanding to the surface of his brown-green, gold-flecked eyes. Most of the time, however, he kept them shut, the papery, quivering lids shielding his fright and the well-known, willful, run-away-filly expression seemed transposed to the unshaven face of a stranger. A new regime was decreed: the patient was to be moved to a rehabilitation center: The next circle of hell was entered.

The route to the hospital was abandoned, and, like loyal camp followers, Ann, Henrietta (now fifteen years old), and I learned the way to the new institution. Here the horrors increased. A bare, drafty barrack had succeeded the cocoon of the hospital. On the first day I was confronted by the army of the maimed, in the corridor in disarray but ready to be commanded. Equipped with crutches (tilted at different angles like the distorted branches of trees in the aftermath of a hurricane), braces, artificial limbs, wheelchairs, stretchers, walkers—instead of rifles and pistols—this battalion comprised a motley assortment of young, old and middle-aged, of both sexes, subordinate to a staff sergeant in the person of an orderly, blatant in the tactlessness of his bodily completeness. Slightly apart from the rest, a figure, despite the restraint of leather thongs, slumped in his wheelchair. His face, putty-colored, his shock of gray hair, matted and shaggy, he resembled a neglected wolfhound more than a human being. Through his baggy, institutional trousers, held up by safety pins, one could discern the bony outline of his knees; one paralyzed arm rested in a sling, the other, thin as a stick, was gesticulating wildly in a dumb show of protest. I approached the invalid's chair.

Through inarticulate grunts, barkings and gurgles, I could just make out, "Get me out of here! Save me!"

"He always kicks up a fuss. He doesn't want to go to gym," said the orderly-sergeant. "He's a newcomer and he will have to learn like the others that orders are orders. You can wait for him in his room. We won't be long up there."

He pushed the chair—Nicholas still producing

angry barking sounds—into the cavernous elevator. The heavy iron door clanged shut. I walked down the hall toward Nicholas's room and the smell, amalgam of antiseptic, brass polish and linoleum, assailed me: I was back at my first school. The years had dwindled to insignificance, taking with them the passing triumphs and joys of Nicholas's life, no more than match-flames in the dark.

Nicholas's cubicle at the rehabilitation center became his home. He returned there after the racking exertions in the gymnasium, the discouraging speech lessons, the useless sessions at "shop," where, with only one arm, he was expected to have the dexterity he had always lacked with two. Yet, bit by bit, a change was taking place. The protests and whinings became infrequent and Nicholas developed a kind of *corps d'esprit*: the pride the lowliest foot soldier may take in the victories of an army in which he is only an insignificant cog. In his new diction, punctuated by those barkings, grunts, gurgles and incomprehensible syllables, he made himself understood.

"Someday you must come up to the gym," he begged. "You will see how much I have improved. We go, one at a time, and all the rest applaud and cheer. It's very exciting!"

I pictured the straggling battalion, pathetically proud of its grotesque feats. Its hopefulness would fill the spectator with pity too strong to be disguised. I never found the courage to go.

"Next week," I promised; but, although Nicholas continued to insist, the day did not arrive.

The initial complaints concerning his meager quarters ceased also. He who had always insisted on the most luxurious suites at the "Ritz"—the world over—appeared resigned to his cubicle. True, Ann, Henrietta and I furnished it with magazines and newspapers, the paper rat's nest in which he felt at ease.

During my visits I often glanced, surreptitiously, at my watch, longing to be set free, while attending absently to his monologues. Nicholas never required answers.

"Don't you think Henrietta has grown very pretty?" he would ask. "Perhaps no beauty, but certainly pretty. She will make someone a wonderful wife, a perfect little homemaker. I hope she will have lots of children." Then, remembering his impecuniousness, which he never really believed in, he added, "Maybe she should think of a career, a hotel school, Cornell is the best. She is so competent. . . ."

My mind wandered during these indistinct mumblings, but my eyes were often caught by an object on the night table. Ann had brought it to him at Christmas in a shopping bag filled with ten-cent store trinkets—a clear plastic block with inserted family photographs of other holiday seasons. Next to an elaborate Christmas tree Nicholas and Ann appeared, looking handsome and jolly, surrounded by pyramids of elaborate gifts. This object remained by his bed in all the institutions to the day of his death. It reminded me of the crystal ball of the fortune teller on the boardwalk at Atlantic City, but it reflected a fabulous past rather than a nebulous future. In Nicholas's room at the rehabilitation center it served to make yesterday come true.

Another side of the cube showed Henrietta in a new, formal riding habit.

"She was the proudest little girl in all Westchester County," Nicholas reminisced.

I winced at his banal sentimentality, which always turned me to stone. But it was not Nicholas's way to notice the mood of another.

Time plays tricks. Things, once eschewed, may become indispensable, while a goal fervently wished for, when attained, often turns to dust, and we ask ourselves why it had ever appeared in a rosy glow of desirability. So, with Nicholas. That first day when he had implored me to "save" him, to get him out, was forgotten. And when the top general, the director of the institute—a personage so mighty and inaccessible that to the inmates and their families his word resounded like that of an invisible deity—ordered my brother to leave, Nicholas mustered his feeble forces to reverse the decision. We all begged, in vain. The patient would progress no further, the center was not meant for incurables. I never knew whether Nicholas was aware of this harsh diagnosis; at any rate, he was forced to submit, to cede his place to some other soldier more able than himself. The next move would be a nursing home. High Hill was to be sold, Ann had no money for the care that Nicholas required around the clock and there would be no room for any help in the cramped two-bedroom apartment for which she was looking. Debts, unpaid for years, menaced

Nicholas from all sides. His sick-leave pay from the advertising firm had ceased. He was bankrupt. My husband and I would have to pay for the nursing home. He alone remained optimistic. Just as the eye cannot endure a direct gaze into the sun, Nicholas, all his life, had avoided facing painful reality.

"Wait and see," he reassured us now, "James Hogan is my friend and the firm cannot do without me—my advertising contacts are too valuable. . . ."

In the meantime, his Baby Ann and his daughter were left to manage unassisted. For Henrietta, giving up her horse was like a preview of future bereavement. But on her visits to the center she stolidly hid her grief. Sitting by Nicholas's invalid's chair, as blond, blue-eyed, snub-nosed and fair-complexioned as he could wish, she listened quietly to his extravagant plans for the future: the next horse would be even better, a prize–winning thoroughbred. And he vowed that he would save High Hill; they would not lose their home. He was unselfconscious about his condition and lavished physical demonstrations of affection on Henrietta, encircling her with his one good arm and kissing her again and again with lips always wet from the saliva oozing out of the paralyzed side of his mouth like uncontrollable tears. She showed no disbelief in his promises, nor did she flinch from his infirmities—the ugly utterances of his discourse, the drooling embraces, the shriveled, helpless limbs. Henrietta accepted them with the matter-of-factness of a child. But her solicitude seemed unnaturally adult, as strange to me as the tiny gold cross, revealed by her open shirt collar, on the smooth, creamy white triangle of her young flesh.

At the rehabilitation center Hugo Merz, marketing analyst for Brandt and Hogan, was a frequent caller. He was respected in that medium, a learned citizen among its "scientists," "economists," "writers," "artists," "philosophers," "psychologists"— a nation identified not by geographical borders but by a value system more idiosyncratic than that of any foreign land. My brother was able to function there; he understood the language. I did not and, as in my childhood, I was grateful for differences that seemed to separate us. Though I despised advertising, I was relieved that Nicholas was so enthusiastically accepted by one of its most prominent practitioners. Hugo Merz would sit by the bedside or next to the wheelchair and his polished horn-rimmed glasses glinted with what appeared to be an intelligence of their own. Every time he shifted his considerable weight, his corpulence threatened the spindling barrack seat. As he talked calmly, with self-assurance, it seemed that the array of numbers lodged behind his high forehead required his whole ponderous body to support them. He wore the conventional dark businessman's suit and Brooks Brothers shirt but his technical erudition lent him professorial distinction, an aura of hairy tweed, leather elbow patches and pipe. When my brother spoke, articulating his words with so much difficulty, Hugo Merz would listen respectfully, not forgetting that Nicholas was, after all, the genius of promotional ideology who had brought forth the unique, the immortal Meistersinger Girl.

The Smythe-Wilson nursing home displayed a bland, moneyed facade. No expense had been spared: ivy grew profusely over rosy brick walls, the white-painted trim shone like enamel on windows and doors, the lawns were green and neat as the felt on billiard tables. The lobby, always supplied with generous bouquets of fresh flowers, was furnished comfortably in familiar home–like eighteenth-century English reproductions. No sign proclaimed, "Abandon hope all ye who enter here." But this thought had been expressed by a cheerful young nurse.

"They usually die soon after they hit this place," she said to me with the indifference of a florist who tells you that a certain bloom will perish in the steam-heated atmosphere of an apartment building.

Yet, Nicholas raved about the luxury of his new surroundings. "It's exactly like the Beverly Hills Hotel!"

He did not, however, relinquish the fight to get back to the rehabilitation center. Despite the material comforts of the Home, deep inside he admitted its underlying purpose—or, rather, lack of purpose. And he missed the crude, barren barrack that stood for progress. In his determination to return he enlisted the names of influential acquaintances, close or distant; he implored them to "pull wires" on his behalf. But the director-deity remained firm, the answer was an invariable no.

So we, the faithful, pursued the route to the nursing home. We soon saw that this institution was the most hideous circle of hell yet. Nicholas, only fifty-five, was the youngest patient and, it seemed, the only one with any of his wits. His cheerfulness had dampened into despondence and defying rules: he refused to leave his room and socialize with the other so-called ambulatory patients.

But it was not in his nature to relinquish all hope. One of the big deals he had hinted at did surface in the newspapers, but he received no remuneration. Had he remained at his post at the advertising agency, increased prestige would have been his only reward. At the nursing home he read the news story again and again, as though visualizing his own invisible portrait, enlarged, behind the print that made no mention of his part in the negotiations. Sitting beside his high hospital bed I helped him compose a letter to the president, the same man whose careworn face I remembered from the dinner party at Nicholas's house. He was still traveling from city to city, joyless, self-important and pitiless, deaf to my brother's pleas that he be kept on the payroll in a minor way until he could return to the office. As we worked over the wording, it was I who felt humiliated. Why could he never give up, accept the inevitable? And in my buried and unformulated consciousness, there was a more acute discomfort engendered by the tacit teachings of our kind to which Nicholas and I had been exposed together: *caution, moderation, observance of interdictions.* A Jew must never press himself or his wares upon an unwilling, advantaged Gentile; precautions defied by my brother again and again. At any rate, those letters, composed and recomposed with so much effort, and without a trace of animosity on his part, were never answered.

One day, on my way to visit Nicholas, passing an open door, I glimpsed a woman flat on her back; emaciated, balding, she gazed fixedly at a cage in which a canary trilled its tiny song without cease. The moribund patient, her toothless mouth open, pointed chin raised, seemed to be drinking in the notes, one by one, as though they were the final elixir of life itself. I hurried on and from that time, as though my safety depended on it, I tried not to look either right or left, but directed my attention strictly downward at the figures in the carpet.

I usually found Nicholas talking long–distance on the telephone. The instrument cradled under his chin, in his thick difficult speech he carried on endless business conversations throughout the United States and overseas. I was familiar with those sham schemes of his, and knowing that my husband and I would have to pay the bills, I often lost all restraint, forgetting Nicholas's plight, shouting at him to stop deluding himself and squandering other people's money. The cruel words tasted bitter on my lips and, after I had recovered myself, the aftertaste of pity and remorse was even more bitter.

Oddly, these outbursts had an unexpected effect on Nicholas; he appeared pleased rather than hurt. And, on a subsequent visit, I would discover him, unregenerate, talking to Istanbul. Ignoring my presence, he continued at length. Finally, replacing the telephone with his good arm, he turned to me. "Don't worry. I have a huge deal under way. I will see that you get a generous cut. We may make millions. Your investment in me will be repayed many times over."

I wanted to believe him, less because of the money than for the sake of his self-respect and mine, too, which remained linked to him, despite my reluctance. But failing credulity, my rage rose again, uncontrollable and futile as in my childhood, while Nicholas regarded me with a strange look in which relief mingled with pleasure. It must be something more than imperviousness, good nature or insensitivity. All at once I thought of that birthday cake that my brother had tactlessly presented to our dying father; like it, my cutting treatment might be reassurance that he was not so very ill, after all, and for this reason it was more soothing to his unspoken terror of death than the gentle consideration of others. My outbursts shattered, for the moment, the mortuary stillness of the nursing home, where the rubber-soled footsteps of the patrolling nurses were muffled by the deep-pile carpeting, the rolling carts bearing multicolored pills arrived silently at the patients' doors, and the faint moans of the dying were all but inaudible behind thick walls.

Once, arriving at Nicholas's room, I found it empty and was told that he was in the lounge. Perhaps, at last, he had found a companion! He had mentioned a woman. She was only in her seventies and

Nicholas had said, "She has a mansion in Newport and her own private plane and pilot!"

I carefully refrained from telling him that I frequently discovered her seated before a typewriter, composing, an attendant informed me, imaginary letters to the Library of Congress concerning copyrights for the "two thousand" books she had never written.

But when I reached the lounge I saw a group of men in dark business suits with my brother in his wheelchair in their midst. Afterward, I found out that it was a syndicate planning to take over a defunct brewery in Detroit. When Nicholas went there himself, he told me, his renown was such that he had been wheeled through the plant to the wild cheers of the workers. "Just as though I were a restored monarch," and there were tears in his eyes as he recalled his reception. But I imagined that the familiar smell of malt in the brewhouse must have been as welcome to him as the aroma of home cooking to a traveling salesman, after the synthetic fare of cafeterias and drugstores and the loneliness of the road. I never knew what went wrong with the brewery in Detroit. On looking back, I believe that the group was composed of shady entrepreneurs who had seized as a disguise upon the solid name of Bloch, caring nothing for Nicholas's pitifully maimed person, expendable as an old rag doll.

Nicholas entered High Hill for the last time on a hot July day; the occasion was Henrietta's sixteenth birthday. The nursing home had released him for the afternoon and Ann had called to invite me to join them for a tea party. No purchaser for the house had turned up yet and my brother's wife and daughter lived on there as caretakers of a haunted past.

We sat in the suffocating heat of the den, Ann, Nicholas, Henrietta, her latest boyfriend and I. The upholstery was now in shreds, the leather chairs rent by gaping wounds. Nicholas was placed on the old sofa, which had been covered by gray sacking like a shroud. Only he appeared cheerful, unabashed by his shocking appearance and his garbled, mumbling speech. He entertained the young man with fabricated accounts of happy prep school days, and comforted his wife and daughter with visions of himself at the helm of the Detroit brewery, at which time he would take the house off the market. By then he would be well again and "Baby Ann," "Baby Henrietta," the decrepit dog and cat would resume life as before. He had forgotten the domestic battles, chiefly concerning his spendthrift ways and the fact that once Ann had even left him, taking Henrietta with her. But, less steely than Margo, not wild like Ramona, she soon succumbed to his bulldozer tactics, returning to High Hill and further dissension. This afternoon Ann looked unusually melancholy and constrained. I had rarely seen her during the daytime dressed in anything but her abbreviated tennis garb, her hair tied back with a bit of scarlet yarn. Now only the freckles dusting her cheekbones like motes in a ray of sun filtered through lowered shades were reminders of the outdoors and the abandoned court where she had found release.

As Nicholas continued to boast of the improvement in his health and the progress of the mythical deal, no one dared to catch anyone else's eye. Henrietta was subdued, Ann preoccupied, probably overwhelmed by bill collectors and her imprisonment in the disintegrating house with its leaking roof, broken plumbing, hanging plaster and the neglected tennis court and swimming pool. And I, filled with pity, fretting at my connection to this wreck in a red-and-white check, open-necked sport shirt, viewed the birthday party as I would the scene of a violent accident. Only Henrietta's friend was able to keep up with Nicholas's cheerful chatter. High Hill had no history for him. It was just old and shabby and Henrietta was young and desirable.

Nicholas was demanding another slice of birthday cake, forbidden fare as he was a diabetic and his doctors believed that this disease which he had ignored for years from fear, gluttony and stubbornness had caused the fatal stroke. Holding the fork in his functioning hand and lowering his putty-colored face toward the plate he ate greedily. "Your Bow-Wow loves chocolate cake," he said, addressing Ann.

Suddenly Nicholas suspended his eating. "Why aren't you using my mother's gold-rimmed Wedgwood china?" he asked Ann.

"I sold it," she said, a robber confessing theft.

"You shouldn't have done that." A veil of sadness passed over his pallid, distorted face. "She always brought it out for 'occasions'; I remember the way the table looked set for a party. . . ."

Why did these words have an even more violent effect on me than the baby talk, the boasting, the willful screams? They were even more disturbing than the ruinous uncontrollable spending. Why did I have to restrain myself from running away from those sentimental evocations of childhood?

The "party china" contained a message for me, also. I used to imagine that it had issued a flashing gold-and-white treasure out of the gloomy recesses of the brownstone where my mother had grown up. It had formed part of her marriage dowry and I, as well as Nicholas, had once admired the gala plates placed at regular intervals along the tables with the cut-crystal goblets and the fluted silver shells containing salted almonds. They were all part of the ritual of entertaining and as necessary to our household as the rich churchly ceremonials are to an observing Christian. To this day the brown, toasty taste of salted almonds tells me in a ghostly, festive whisper, "There will be guests to dinner tonight." These random, inconsequential memories of mine were often shared by my brother—and by him alone. We had a common past and no matter how vehemently I might rattle the chains of consanguinity that bound us I never succeeded in breaking them.

Like the rumble of thunder, the sound of wheels on the driveway announced the arrival of the ambulette that was to take the patient back to the nursing home. Two orderlies in white appeared in the doorway.

"No, no, I won't go," Nicholas protested. I waited nervously for the retchings and screams that would follow. But they would avail him nothing now and the men in white lifted him, weightless, from the sofa. I looked away; it was unbearable to see him being stowed inside the vehicle, dragged away from the home he loved. We stood in the driveway to see him off. And he called out the window, "I'll be back! Wait and see. Soon we'll all be together again."

But he never did return; his health deteriorated along with his spirits and the strong will that all his life had helped him attain the possible and, also, to try for the impossible. His determination snapped when he was forced to sign the papers for the sale of High Hill. Nicholas could surmount bankruptcy, the loss of parents and wives, but to be homeless —that he could not survive. When I visited him now, I was greeted with monotonous complaints about the nursing home where he obdurately continued to disobey all rules and regulations. He never discussed his business projects anymore, even his saccharine recollections of childhood ceased. It seemed that only the vagaries of his bowels were of interest to him. It was unbearable and I even longed for those costly calls to Istanbul, Paris or London. . . . Visitors to the sickroom had grown sparse, like the poinsettia plant that had somehow survived transplantation from the rehabilitation center to the nursing home, but having shed its spiky petals, it remained on the windowsill, a bare, tough stalk supporting a few leaves in a pot covered by tinfoil.

Hugo Merz visited the nursing home only rarely, as did the friends and employees from the brewery.

I used to feel comforted, my responsibility lightened by their numbers gathered around the wheelchair at the center.

However, Nicholas continued to have one loyal, regular visitor, Chip Middlemarch, whom I had met at dinner at High Hill. Handsome, with his burnished helmet of auburn hair, his glowing health resplendent next to the sagging flesh and brittle bones entombed in the nursing home, when he entered the sickroom where Nicholas lay on his bed, his vigor was like a gust of mountain air. Only he could rouse Nicholas, who with the aid of walker, braces and his friend's strong arms, would wobble down the corridor with Chip murmuring words of encouragement like a mother to a toddler. Nicholas had a champion, a descendant of the small, tow-headed boy with the pugnacious fists in the schoolyard long ago. Yet again, oddly, my brother appeared to take his loyal Sancho Panza for granted. His fertile brain had always been occupied by finding means to storm the barricades of the people who spurned him, the places where he was not accepted. Accustomed to opprobrium, it was as though those who stood by him were devalued by the very fact of their devotion. The restricted schools and clubs that refused him, the pinnacles of business never scaled, the scornful women, the unbending deities like the director of the rehabilitation center and the pitiless Hogan (whom he continued to bombard with unanswered letters)—these were his goals. I watched his progress down the hall. Held up by steel appliances, with his gigantic height, he reminded me of the Eiffel Tower tilted to the precarious angle of the Tower of Pisa and animated to resemble a perambulating human being.

Yet with a ray of his old optimism he crowed, "Watch me! I'm walking!"

His days at the Smythe-Wilson nursing home were coming to an end. His noisy complaints and insubordination, combined with the high cost of keeping him there, occasioned the final move. At his last asylum, the most alien of them all, Nicholas found a modicum of repose. It was a ramshackle shingle two-family house with a homely glassed-in porch where the patients who were well enough to come downstairs were treated to a view of a rundown suburban street. But, unlike Smythe-Wilson, where routine was adhered to with impersonal frigidity, this boardinghouse for the moribund was run, in its slovenly fashion, by love. Filipo and Maria Silvano, the owners, resembled a couple escaped from a circus freak show: he, a virtual dwarf, swarthy and agile as a monkey; she, of gargantuan, uncorseted girth, with dyed red hair and coquettish curls. "No one can give a backrub like Filipo. He is better than any masseur!" my brother reported. As for Maria Silvano, she mothered Nicholas without restraint. He turned to her as once he had relied upon the care of the very different Mrs. Jones, his "Mauress," the guardian of our childhood ills. In the rickety wooden house he was able to hear Mrs. Silvano's heavy, lumbering tread everywhere, the sound of her voice, and he was less lonely. When she stopped to chat with him, he no longer felt obliged to pretend to be adult, but with an inaudible sigh of relief, sank into the dependency of an infant, as into the billowy depths of a down pillow. His quarters, however, contained no such luxury: furnished in total austerity with a chipped white-painted iron bedstead, a filing cabinet to hold the patient's few belongings, one tattered armchair. Although Ann, Henrietta and I brought flowers, he barely glanced at them. All day his eyes were fixed on a brass plaque on the wall facing his bed. It had been awarded him in his absence and it was engraved by the Brewers' Association of America with his name as an honorary member. It reminded Nicholas that he was the inheritor of family history; he dreamed of the lost paradise of the Meistersinger Brewery in the days when he was president. It was sold now to a manufacturer of peanuts and the disintegrating remains of the plant in Bushwick had been taken over by a factory dealing in cheap knitted goods. The industrious nineteenth-century business, an entire world in miniature, existed only in my brother's recall. With his demise, it would disappear for me as though it had never been. All else seemed to have dwindled for Nicholas: he no longer addressed those pleas to the implacable Hogan; modern advertising techniques did not interest him anymore. Even his "Baby Ann" and his beloved Henrietta were growing remote.

His Catholicism had lost its importance, also. Although Father Phelan lurked around the Silvanos' nursing home, like a benevolent bird of prey, waiting to seize upon some soul about to be liberated from the body, he knocked upon my brother's door in vain. At his approach, Nicholas would scream, "Don't let him in! Keep him out of here!"

I was never sure whether his reaction was due to the repudiation, at the end, of his borrowed faith, a return to the family creed of atheism. It was true that his room contained no vestige of the Catholic religion, no relic, crucifix or holy picture—only that brass plaque riveting his dimming gaze. I think it more likely, however, that Father Phelan's presence, in his long black cassock, meant the approach of the total darkness that Nicholas still fought off with what little was left of his indomitable will. But the priest's stubbornness vied with my brother's and he returned daily. Sometimes it was I who was delegated to chase him and his offerings of churchly consolation away. So far as I know, as long as consciousness remained to him my brother refused the ritual of the last rite. The instinctive denial of death by the human organism, no matter how wrecked, had proved stronger than the established church. In February, in the middle of the night, one week short of his fifty-seventh birthday, Nicholas died, alone at Silvanos' nursing home.

The funeral was large—with many people I did not recognize—at the local Catholic church he had attended. There were also figures from my submerged past struggling out of an obliterating fog. The Bloch cousins were there en masse: the very same who had attempted to oust Nicholas from the brewery. With the family business gone, they had dispersed, coming together now with solemn, grieving faces, as though their hostility to the deceased had never existed. Maybe my brother *was* mourned by his relatives in death, even though he had been disliked by them in life. Friends from our circle, out of touch with Nicholas since youth, all turned out: they shivered at the specter of their own mortality uncovered by the death of a contemporary. René de la Riviere, sleek and somber, his eyes decorously lowered, was indifferent to his part in the downfall of Meistersinger, former secretaries and old family retainers sobbed unrestrainedly. James Hogan lent his severe presence. Despite my resentment of him, I could not help wishing that somehow Nicholas would know he was there; it would have given my brother pleasure to believe that, at the end, the impregnable bastion had been stormed. Before the service everyone congregated in an antechamber that held the open coffin. It was my first sight of a corpse and I was grateful to a strange woman kneeling before it, hiding it from my view. I choked on the heavy scent of flowers dying in the airless room. At last the woman rose and, making the sign of the cross, moved off. My brother was revealed to me. He was covered to the waist and laid out in his old blue school blazer. His face with all care and illness expunged looked youthful. Even the large pale birthmark on the high bridge of his nose had been obliterated through the skill of the undertaker's art. But I was aware of it beneath the paint. I knew how many times he had had this branding removed only to discover that it had reappeared, ineradicable as the writing on a palimpsest. His eyelids were smooth and innocent. Here, in place of my brother, was a knight—not a picaresque Don Quixote—but a handsome Lancelot I had never known. Suddenly I was engulfed by regret, a feeling of irretrievable waste. My brother was gone. Who was he? The question would always remain unanswered.

The service was held in the main nave of the church, so spacious that it reduced the mourners who had appeared numerous in the antechamber to a mere handful, insignificant as driftwood thrown upon dark wet sand. Afterward, those closest to the deceased filed out into the rainy winter day to the burial ground at the rear of the church. We stood beside the grave, a little knot of people, all in black, with black umbrellas dripping steadily. The priest said a prayer at graveside. Each of us dropped a rose, provided by the undertaker, upon Nicholas's final home. As we returned to the waiting cars I lingered behind to read the names on the headstones: FOGARTY, DUFFY, MCGOVERN, FUSSELLI —soon Nicholas Bloch would be added to their number. In spite of all still a Jew, the only one in this homogeneous Catholic community, an outsider in death as he had been in life—lonely and apart.

A stab of abandonment pierced me. I was now the last living member of my childhood family. Why, then, had I tried to jettison Nicholas? I realized, too late, that it was chiefly because of my own lack of self–confidence: his oddness, his conspicuousness, had heightened my own unease at being Jewish.

But my attempts had failed, it is impossible to rupture the links that have been forged in blood. The fears we shared had caused us both to shrink from our heritage in the vain struggle to melt altogether into the host nation. My personal rejection of Nicholas was related to the unspoken aims of my family, itself a microcosm, a concentric circle within the greater sphere of assimilationists who, in turn, are no more than a sect, a mere detour in endless time: the history of Jewish survival.

MCGUSTY, FITZGERALD, O'CONNOR. I continued to study the names above the graves—"Adams, Albright, Baker, Bloch, Campbell . . . Cohen." Now it was the echo of my father's voice out of the past that I was hearing. We were in our suite aboard the *S.S. Berangaria* and he was reading the passenger list aloud. When he came to "Cohen," he had paused and when he continued there was a hint of distaste in his voice. Another Jew on the satisfactory Christian roll call—I moved out of the cemetery, leaving the grave with its secrets, accompanied by the burden of an unresolved relationship.

Brother